Blown Away

Blown Away

Anadi Naik

BLACK EAGLE BOOKS

2019

 BLACK EAGLE BOOKS

7464 Wisdom Ln,
Dublin, OH 43016, USA
E-mail: info@blackeaglebooks.org
Website: www.blackeaglebooks.org

First International Edition published by
Black Eagle Books, 2019

Blown Away by Anadi Naik

Cover & Interior Design: Ezy's Publication

Library of Congress Control Number: 2019943160
ISBN- 978-1-64560-015-2 (Paperback)

Printed in United States of America

To
Tapu

Acknowledgment

My heartfelt thanks to:

Ambassador (retired) Dr. Har Swarup Singh for his critical reading of the manuscript.

Dr. Krishna Banaudha and Dr. Sita Gupta for their encouragement at various stages.

Mr. Satya Pattanaik for converting the manuscript into a book.

My wife Carroll without whose help the project would not have been possible.

- Anadi Naik

1

Jhumpi was married at age 13 and had her first child when she was just over 14. And by her mid twenties she was a widow with two young children. She had no savings to fall back on. There was no life insurance to talk about. Her family had a piece of land she did not know where it was. As a married woman she knew her place was inside the house, literally. She never stepped out of her immediate neighborhood. Feeding her children, cooking for her husband and family and taking care of all the pujas and festivities were her job and she took each of them seriously.

Until her husband's death Jhumpi was a pampered woman. At home there was plenty of food to eat and oil to cook with. Her husband made sure that they did not run out of staple. While the monsoon rain continued for days or when flash floods from the river drowned almost everything in the village. She wore silver bangles on both wrists as every day's ornaments but saved her gold bangles for special occasions. When the occasion was over, she hid her gold bangles in a wooden chest locked from outside. Her husband was an educated man. In those days there was no school in the village. Yet he had gone to Puri, a distant town full of temples and learning institutions – and educated himself in the ancient language Sanskrit. He knew astrology and all kinds of Sanskrit verses. People from around many miles came to seek out his advice on things important such as finding an auspicious day to negotiate a son's or daughter's wedding. He advised them about the right moments to draw the map to build a new house. He calculated an auspicious evening to celebrate a married daughter's first menstruation. Those days, girls as young as 5 or 7 years old were being married. But until their menstruation they stayed with their parents. This gave a kind of social insurance to the girls. If anything happened to their parents then they could move into their already arranged in-law's house. That was the logic.

Jhumpi's husband was a respected man in the village. He did not have a whole lot of money but an unusual amount of respect. Compared to many of his neighbors her family was well off. They had a house. They had food. Above all they could afford a cow that gave them milk from which they could make curd and then all kinds of cheese and yogurt.

But her husband's death changed all that. Soon after he died their immediate neighbors thought she, as a widow with two young children, was going to be a noose around their neck. Many of them acted standoffish. Others expressed sympathy but in a roundabout way let this be known that they could not help feed the family. She did not know how jealous some of her relatives were of her when she was well off and her husband was still living. Now it came out in the open. She overheard one of her relatives saying

"Why do I have to bother about her? She never gave me anything". It was cruel. But Jhumpi had no time to dwell on such a small meanness.

She could not rely on her brother as he had six children of

his own. As a village priest, he did not make a lot of money. His situation was always hand to mouth. When her husband was living she quite often used to "lend" her brother money and rice with full expectation that the loan was never going to be paid back. The siblings loved each other very much. She was sure that if her brother were well off he would take her and her children into his family. But knowing his financial situation Jhumpi could not rely on him. She had an 11year old son who was her biggest asset.

Jhumpi's gold bangles and silver bangles were useless now. As a widow she did not need any bangles or ornaments. She could not wear them. The ornaments, like the red dot used to adorn her forehead, were the stuff for women with husbands. Now she had no need to wear any of them. There was no income. Whatever grains and savings her husband had accumulated, most of it was used in his funeral and the mourning ceremony.

Friends and relatives came to her husband's funeral. All of them seemed to be genuine in their condolence. They expressed sympathy and sorrow. It seemed to her that all of them were very much fond of her husband. Their sympathy gave her solace and strength. After all of them were gone, she had to face the reality around her. Her children needed food. Her son needed education. Come summer, she had to buy straw to thatch her roof. Otherwise the monsoon rain would pour into her kitchen. The immediate neighbors and relatives could not be counted on for financial help.

Her husband's death broke her heart. Inside her, she had a terrible feeling of emptiness and sadness. But she could not be too obvious about her inner despair. She needed to make her children strong. So she outwardly had to show strength.

As a practical matter, the first thing Jhumpi did was sell the piece of land that was in her husband's name. As a widow she had no right to her husband's real property. According to the law of the time, ownership of the land belonged to the male child. In her case the male child was a minor. She had to get special permission to sell her husband's land. Since the buyer was an influential man from a nearby village, there was no difficulty in doing so. Besides, the man was paying only one third of the land's market value. In spite of his cheating, Jhumpi was thankful to him that he was kind enough to buy her land. With whatever money she got from the sale she bought food and necessities for her children.

The money did not last very long.

After a while she sold the silver rings for her toes. She sold her silver broach and lace. The day she sold her gold bangles she felt as if someone pushed a needle down her heart. She wanted to cry at that moment but could not. She had saved her gold for her daughter to be given as a present at the time of her wedding.

When the girl got married, she had planned to hand her the gold. Now that possibility was gone! It made her sad - very sad.

Like the money from the sale of land, the money from the silver and gold lasted a few months. That year she was able to thatch the roof of the house. The following year, it was difficult. She could not buy any straw for the roof.

The pieces of exposed bamboos on the rooftop attracted monkeys. Unaware of Jhumpi's condition below, they jumped from her roof to trees and from trees to her roof and then somewhere else. When it rained, there was hardly a spot in her house that was dry. To catch rainwater inside, she and her children used all kinds of earthen pots. The water leaked in so many places that they did not have enough earthen pots to place under the leaks. She and her children had to huddle in a corner and try to sleep at night while still squatting there.

"God, when is it going to end?" she would ask God with whom she seemed to be very angry. She could not fall asleep. All night she would be busy emptying the pots. Tears would silently flow from her eyes but she would not sob in case her children caught her doing that.

Jhumpi's only son Harish had to grow up fast. A year after his father's death at age 12 the boy had to take over some of the family business such as planting a few pumpkin plants to spread over the rooftop. He had to do the marketing for his mother and sister. Whenever there was something in the village that needed representation from his family, he would volunteer. More and more his mother used him to get all the support she needed. At the same time she demanded a full report on everything from her son.

By the grace of God, Jhumpi's pumpkins that year seemed to grow much bigger than anybody's in the village. She would send her son to market to sell a couple of them. But Harish Sharma was not very savvy in his bargaining skills. He would sell the vegetable to the first customer at whatever price he was offered. Having had no money at home, the very sight of it would thrill him. He would come home to show the loot to his mother. Jhumpi would see the money. She would be upset with the inept business practices of her son. Then she would remember that her son was only a boy! At that instant, she would curse loudly at the customer who cheated her son. But in her heart of hearts she would be happy realizing that now she had a few pennies that she could spend on her children.

Jhumpi, toward the end of the second year of her widowhood, managed to buy a calf. Actually, a neighbor in the village was selling his cow to a Muslim businessman who intended to take it to a slaughter- house. The cow was too old to produce anymore calves and its milking had ended. The neighbor's wife died recently. After completing the wedding of his only daughter, he wanted to become a Sadhu – an ascetic with no worldly possessions. Other than the cow he and his wife did not own anything. Their hut was on a piece of land that belonged to another person. Before he left home to embrace the life of an ascetic he wanted to leave some money to his daughter. That is why he sold the cow. He knew that the animal was destined for a slaughterhouse. The cow was old and useless. No one had any need for it. But its calf was young and full of possibilities. The man could not, as a good Hindu, send it to be killed. When Jhumpi came to know that the man was willing to sell his calf, she offered him a bit of money. The man was a former student of her husband and called Jhumpi "aunt". Everybody in the village seemed to call her aunt.

There was no bargaining between them. In front of another man from the village Jhumpi gave the seller whatever money she had saved from her pumpkin sales. Then she offered a few blades of green grass to the calf. Thus the transaction was complete and the calf came to her house.

Her son Harish did some errands for a shopkeeper. That way he had the first opportunity to select from all the damaged and rejected goods of the shop. By the age of 13 he had an education up to the 5th grade. This qualified him to teach ABCs to 4 and 5 year olds. The parents of the little children under his charge gave rice and money at the end of the month as his fee. When there was a special occasion such as a wedding in the family, or a Puja or some kind of celebration, they brought him sweets and coconut. He taught all day – from early in the morning to late in the afternoon. For a few hours the children and he left for a dip in the village pond and then home to eat their mid-day meals.

After finishing teaching for the day, young Harish Sharma went to get grass for the calf. By nightfall daily he was able to collect a load of green grass.

Jhumpi made sure that her calf ate well. In addition to her own, she regularly collected rice-water and left over gruel from the neighbors and fed it to her animal. Within a year the calf was ready to be pregnant. The day the young animal started spreading her hind legs and mooed in desperation Jhumpi realized that the calf was in heat. She asked her son to fetch the village bull. The bull was in the other end of the village. It took some prodding and half a basket of grass to bring him to the intended location. As soon as the bull heard the moo from the calf he came straight toward her. No prodding was required. All day, Jhumpi continued to pray for a successful pregnancy for her dear calf. She was boundlessly happy when the bull did its job. The calf became pregnant.

For the next nine months Jhumpi fed the animal the right amount of husk, gruel and grass. There was always the fear for the young cow's miscarriage. Therefore, she had to be very careful in feeding it. In the mean time she and her daughter made patties from the cow dung and dried the patties in the back yard under the sun. Every morning they managed to dry a handful of patties. When a dozen or so of those were accumulated, she sold them. The price of her patties depended on the person on the other end as well as her financial urgency. She could not be too adamant about the price or businesslike in her dealings with her neighbors! Some bought from her on credit.

Finally, a male calf was born after a long wait of nine months. When the calf hit the ground after separating from its mother's womb, it lay on the ground for a short moment. The first thing it did was stand up and then started running in a daze. At that moment, Jhumpi's happiness seemed to be boundless. She foresaw her radiant future. A male calf is pricier than a female calf. Within two years the male calf can be ready to become a bullock. For tilling the land or pulling a cart a bullock is very much needed. So she can sell the male calf as soon as the cow becomes dry – she envisioned silently. She hoped to get some real money.

Her daughter Sumi helped her in cleaning and cooking. Her son taught ABCs to the children of the village. She devoted all her time around the cow. She fed the cow and the calf and made sure they never lacked any grass in their feeding basket made from fibers of bamboo. Three times a day – in the morning, the afternoon and in the evening she offered both of them rice water and rice gruel mixed with rice husk. The animals loved their diet. Often she would pet and caress the underside of their necks. She would always leave a big pot of water for them to drink.

From the cow's fermented milk Jhumpi made curd, yogurt, butter and cheese. From butter she made ghee. For this product to be made, she had to do hours of churning of the fermented milk known as Dahi. Then she had to collect butter from the churned milk. In a very low fire she would let the butter sit for hours to become ghee. This rarified butter would be used to make offerings to various Gods and Goddesses. On religious occasions, of which there was one or two every month, Jhumpi would fill a brass lamp with ghee and then place a fresh wicker in it and take the lamp to the temple that stood at the end of the village.

This temple – the only brick structure in the village - had a big circular room protected by a thatched roof. In the center of the room, there was a sandstone sculpture of a big penis representing lord Shiva, the destroyer of the world. There are many stories that circulate in the village about how this statue arrived in the village. One of them is the following that everyone seemed to believe:

A milky cow from the other side of the river kept coming to the spot where the temple is now. Without its calf or the touch of a milkman's hand the cow would empty its udder and the milk from her teats would flow like a waterfall. It so happened that a Sadhu- a holy man - was passing through the village. The Sadhu wore saffron color clothes and had a bushy beard. Wooden thongs with horn and leather stems adorned his feet. The sadhu held his thongs with the gap next to his big toes. When he walked, the wooden thongs vibrated like a small firecracker. He was a man with a very big frame and looked tall and imposing. Before becoming a holy man he might have been a thief or a smalltime crook or a womanizer or one who could not pay his debts. He might have been devout person. But now he was a Sadhu, a holy man. Nobody questioned his authenticity and no one asked him about his past.

When the Sadhu heard about the cow he went to inspect the place himself, alone. As the villagers would later describe it:

The Sadhu saw a snake curled up on the spot that looked a bit raised and grassy. That is where the cow emptied its udder. The snake, the raised spot and the cow's devotion to the place – all of this was a sure sign for him that Lord Shiva who was always adorned with poisonous snakes resided on that spot. He advised the villagers to dig up that area. He had no doubt that the villagers would find the statue of Lord Shiva from under the raised ground. The villagers could not ignore the prodding of a Sadhu especially when there was the question of finding lord Shiva.

On the auspicious morning of the next full moon every household in the village sent a male member to dig up that spot. The work started after puja and consisted of chanting verses from the Vedas, making a small holy fire and breaking a coconut. All the participants had purified themselves by taking a dip in the river nearby and all of them had fasted until the puja was over. In anticipation of unearthing Lord Shiva the spot took the character of becoming holy. The diggers dotted their foreheads with the dusts of this holy ground.

After a few hours they found a two- feet long sand stone as smooth as a baby's bottom. The stone looked like a huge penis. The villagers had no doubt that this was the precious object that they have been looking for. The object represented Lord Shiva. As soon as the stone was found a huge chanting of "Glory to Lord Shiva "went up. The village priest was called in. It being a full-moon- day, a huge celebration took place that afternoon. The village was ecstatic about it.

Every one was thankful to the Sadhu for finding Lord Shiva for their village. Immediately a plan was hatched to find a home for the Lord. In the meantime a consensus was reached to place Him under the banyan tree at the very end of the village. The place instantly became a holy place. The stone became the protector of the village. Men, women, and children bowed their heads before this stone placed under a tree. They asked this stone to fulfill their needs and desires. Married women wished to have sons, marriage age girls each wished to find a good husband, those whose husbands were in far away places like Calcutta or Cuttack to earn a living wished their safe return home, the sick prayed to be cured. All of them in their own way offered puja. Villagers brought in flowers, coconuts and butter for sacrifice. Slowly, the tree and the stone occupied a very prominent place in the life of the village. Both of them became sacred.

The stone could not stay in the open air too long. With the help of the local landlord a brick house was built. Everyone from the village contributed according to his ability. Those who knew how to build a wall or to mix mud to set bricks did so voluntarily. Some carried wood. Some split bamboo to make a pillar. Some tried to build the roof. Other people collected goods for the temple. The work started on an auspicious day in the spring. Before the onset of the monsoon all the work was over and there was a big celebration in the village to open the temple.

Ever since the holy stone was discovered, the entire village wanted the sadhu to stay in the village. He being a holy man every one thought of him very highly. The Sadhu on his part had no family to take care of or any land to till or any cow to graze. He lived by himself totally detached from personal relationships.

Other than two pieces of orange color wrap he owned nothing. By the common practice of a Sadhu he usually slept at night on the outside porch of any family that he came across in any village. Before dawn he usually woke and took a bath in the nearby pond or river. He did his prayers before daybreak. When the sun came out he was always ready to face the new day. He was never sick. And his good health kept him going from place to place. The sadhu never worried about his next meal. All the God-fearing men and women in all the villages he traveled through fed him well. Often he was given so much good food to eat that he distributed it among the children.

Now that the entire village wanted him to stay in the village, the Sadhu could not refuse its request. " If God wants me to stay, I will stay" said the sadhu. The people of the village had no way of knowing the will of God in this case. But they were relieved to see that the holy man did not abandon them. After a few days, they were convinced that the Sadhu was not leaving their village. They felt good about it.

The sadhu on his part became the prime mover as well as the most important force to bring the villagers together to build a house for the deity whom he referred to in Sanskrit as lingum. Lingum means penis. It also depicted Lord Shiva the destroyer. For ordinary villagers it was difficult to comprehend penis with the destruction of the world but they did not want to have an intellectual fistfight with the Sadhu who looked like a learned man. They refused to question what he said. They admired him for his holiness and most importantly, they trusted him.

The project of building a house for the deity also gave the Sadhu a reason to stay in the village. Once the temple was built he could rest there at night. Next to the circular house, the villagers eventually built a small hut for the Sadhu. All the leftover materials from building the temple were used for this purpose.

Once the deity was placed in its sanctuary, it had to be worshipped properly. This required special skills. Besides, worshipping has to be done everyday. The Sadhu was like a roving vagabond. Such an important thing could not be entrusted to him. So the village had to employ a regular worshipper. The people in the village had a common fear that when the God or the Gods became angry they caused all kinds of trouble for human destiny. Through floods, droughts, malaria and smallpox the village had its own share of misfortunes. Therefore its inhabitants did not want to add more misfortune by neglecting the deity of its proper worship. The priest who regularly worshipped the deity and the Sadhu complemented each other.

Whenever the Sadhu came by her house, Jhumpi offered him some milk or curd to drink. He always drank the entire glass in what seemed to be just one gulp. "Auntie, nobody makes curd like you do. Yours is heavenly" the sadhu would comment.

For whatever reason, the Sadhu called Jhumpi "Auntie". In the small village everybody knew everybody. One way or other everyone had to be related to the next person in the village. The relationships were defined as brother, sister, uncle, aunt, grandfather and grandmother. The concept of casual friendship or acquaintance was foreign to village life. Now, Jhumpi became an aunt to the Sadhu and the Sadhu became like a nephew to her. Their mutual relationship gave him a kind of guardianship over her son. If her son did something disagreeable Jhumpi invariably used the Sadhu as a point of reference.

On her part, Jhumpi was always kind to the Sadhu because

he had chosen the path of religiousness. He had renounced worldly possessions. Besides, he had helped to find Lord Shiva and had built the temple for the deity. In her way of thinking this was not a small feat for anybody. She admired his dedication. To her, feeding a holy man was a good thing to do and good deeds were always rewarded in a future life. According to her religious belief a human life came to this world following many past lives. The forms of those lives were shaped according to the deeds done in the life before.

In this life Jhumpi wanted to do as many good things as possible. Taking proper care of the cow and feeding the Sadhu were parts of that plan. In her way of thinking her good deeds were a future insurance for Nirvana where all the cycles of life ended. She did not want to come back to this earth as a cat or a rabbit or a dog. Given all the obstacles of her present life she did not want to come back as a human being either.

In her present life, she felt, God has not treated her well. This must have been due to some wrong things she did in her previous life. In this life she is being punished - she theorized. Jhumpi seemed to have endured plenty of misfortune and grief and heartache. Yet, she was thankful for her blessings also. Her cow was giving milk. Her children were growing up and her son was shouldering household responsibilities like a grown man. This year, she was able to thatch the roof over her head. Unlike many other families in the village she and her children had enough to eat.

Every Monday she would take a jug of milk to the temple to offer to the deity. For her, Monday was an auspicious day. How and why she came to that conclusion she did not know. As long as one can remember, she continued to take her offering every Monday to the temple. She prayed for her children's health, welfare and protection. She was concerned about her son. He seemed to be working too hard. Since his father died, responsibility for every one in the family rested on his shoulder. When Jhumpi would get too worried about this thing or that her son would try to console her. He hated to see his mother weep for any reason.

But weeping came to her naturally. In her own moments of despair she would look at her son with all the concerns of a mother.

"The boy is growing up too fast" – She would mutter to herself silently. She wished her husband were alive today so her son could be spoiled and pampered like other boys in the village.

2

Durgesh Panda and his wife Sati, blessed with two sons and two daughters, enjoyed their blissful lives in a village named Soroda. They had a large tract of farmland that produced all the food their family needed.

Besides looking after his agriculture Durgesh Panda loaned money to other families of Soroda and nearby villages. The business of money lending brought him a handsome profit. Since he was the source of instant cash, no one seemed to have any bad things to say in his own village or other villages. He was known around the area as panda babu which was equivalent to being called Mr. Panda.

Durgesh Panda's eldest son Basu was a school teacher who taught in an elementary school run by the local government in a nearby village. His younger son Bhupa looked after the family land. The young men were hard working and smart The Pandas were very proud of their sons both of whom were now married and lived under the same roof. Their mother Sati Panda was a hard task master. With her loud mouth and absolute intolerance for ill manners she kept everyone in the household in line. That included her husband. She was the only person in the entire village genuinely feared by Durgesh Panda. As the rumor goes, it had something to do with the quantity of dowry she had brought into their marriage.

Sati and Durgesh Panda's two daughters Haru and Paru were by any standard really pretty. Haru was the older one. The girls were each other's best friends. They seemed to be inseparable. Whatever they did they seemed to do together.

The girls learned good manners from their mother. Compared to most other girls in the village they seemed to be a lot more sophisticated. Because their parents had money and in many ways better off Haru and Paru could afford to buy things from the hawkers who occasionally came to their village peddling cosmetics, hair oil, fragrances, bangles and colorful scarves. They wore nice clothes and ornaments while going to a fair or to a function in the village. Unlike other girls of their age they were privileged to learn reading and writing.

A teacher, an elderly man with a straight nose and a long line of sandalwood paste on his forehead, came to their house and the girls, at an early age, learned their ABCs from him. Later on, he taught them stories from different epics. He taught them simple math so that when the girls eventually went to their in-law's house they would be well prepared for the real world. The teacher also taught them how to write letters. In the process the girls were able to read great epics written in their spoken language called Odia. They also learned many ancient stories bearing whatever interpretation the teacher gave to them. Above all, the girls memorized many devotional songs and holy verses. They recited them in evening prayers and on special occasions.

Haru and Paru were born 18 months apart. And they were much younger than their two brothers. Recently, the weddings of their brothers took place a year apart from each other. The girls by then had become young women, sufficiently distant from their childhood. According to the calculation of the mother, both Haru and Paru had learned as much as a girl was supposed to learn in terms of reading and writing. So Sati Panda asked the teacher to stop coming.

Between the two Panda daughters Haru seemed to be the shy one. She did not like to readily show off her knowledge. While visiting a friend's house, if she were asked to read something from a book she would always hesitate and express a lack of confidence to do so. Yet, she had perfect mastery of her reading. Her letter writing skills were good. She knew how to address a letter and how to do the salutation. She also knew how to end her letter with a perfect sentence.

The problem Haru faced while learning to write a letter was that she did not have a friend whom she could write a letter. All her friends lived in Soroda and they were all girls. None of them knew how to read or write. The girls usually helped their mothers and aunts in household chores. They made cow dong patties, chafed husks from rice for cooking and went to collect grass for their family cows. So she had to imagine that her friends lived in Calcutta or Cuttack – the places to which she had never been. She had to write them imaginary letters. In the same way, she thought of her parents and brothers living in Bombay or Delhi. The names of the cities she had only heard. She kept writing letters to them with the pounding heart of a young girl.

Haru came to realize that after sometime girls get married. Instantly, they graduate from girlhood to becoming women. Husbands of some of those women go to distant places to make a living. So the wives had to let the husbands know about goings on through letters. Her teacher had never approached this subject with her. She, on her part, always felt shy to ask him how to address her future husband in a letter. Such an incident in Soroda had never happened before. All the wives were illiterate and hardly any man lived away in a distant city. The whole thing was left to her imagination.

At times Haru worked in her own mind as to how she would start such a letter. " Respected," "Honorable," "Hi," "My dear," "so and so Babu," – a lot of ideas like this came to her mind. But none of these salutations seemed to be the right one. In her subconscious she felt as if something was missing but she did not know what. Finally, after a lot of attempts to find the right word for a salutation she tucked away the issue in the far corner of her mind.

Ever since she turned 12 her parents had been looking for a suitable match for her. At age 13 she had her first menstruation. Then the matter of finding a husband for Haru became urgent for them. Although a search was going on, no one asked her anything about it. In a serious matter like marriage, a girl is not supposed to be consulted. It is an accepted fact that while unmarried, a girl is protected by her parents or guardians. Thereafter, as a married woman, she is protected by her husband or in-laws. A girl just does not have the kind of independence that is accorded to a man or to her brother. Therefore, Haru did not know and was not informed of all the details about her prospective suitors. Her parents acted toward her as if nothing was happening. They were absolutely sure that they were acting in her best interest.

While Sati and Durgesh Panda were worried about finding a suitable groom for Haru, nobody in the family seemed to take Paru seriously. She was the youngest among all her siblings. Everyone in the family continued to treat her like a child. And she took full advantage of it. After her older sister Haru's menstruation the teacher stopped coming to the house. As a result, any further advancement of her education also stopped. The village had no school and she was not allowed to travel to the next village. Now, she had plenty of free time on her hands and she liked it that way. At times she made herself available to overhear things that were being discussed in or around the house. If it was about Haru's marriage then she took more interest in it and tried to overhear as much as she could. That way she was able to deliver all the unvarnished facts to her sister along with her own comments. Although her parents did not tell her about the search for a husband for her, Haru was able to get all the necessary tidbits through her younger sister.

By any yardstick, the Panda family in Soroda was well off. It had the ability to give a proper dowry to its daughter in marriage. This factor did not go unnoticed by the parents or guardians of several prospective grooms. Some of them demanded cash up front. Some wanted a couple of acres of land. Another person wanted a certain amount of gold. Durgesh Panda had enough cash or land or gold that he could have given in a dowry. But the idea itself was repugnant to him. His own pride prevented him to give into any such demand. Asking for money to marry someone's daughter was repugnant to him. He felt as if the groom was being sold! He wanted his daughter to get married on her own merit, not because of the dowry offered by her father. Besides, the other side needed to be the people of proper stature. They need not to be well off. But the family has to be respected in the village. In this regard some of the prospects did not measure up to the Panda family. Their manners, the way they lived, or their family history were not always compatible. Sati Panda had no problem in digging up all the details of these families. As a result the proposals did not materialize.

Haru's mother Sati Panda did not want her daughter to grow up as an old maid. However, her idea of a good son-in-law differed from her husband's. She wanted the young man to come from a well-to-do- family that has a good name in its own village. Preferably, he would know how to manage and deal with servants and sharecroppers. He must be smart enough to know the value of his own land. His education did not matter.

On the other hand Durgesh Panda did not care much about the wealth of his future son-in-law. He was convinced that a man could make his own fortune. All a man needed was a chance. Therefore, he was willing to accept a young man from a poor family as his son-in-law as long as his behavior was not questionable. The young man must have some education, because it brought a man culture and culture was very important to him.

Durgesh Panda was well aware of his position in his own village. He was quite secure and affluent. Therefore, he knew that finding a young man from another family like his own would be difficult. On that point he was perfectly willing to compromise. However, one thing he was adamant about was that the young man must be well versed in Sanskrit. He and his family came from the highest caste in the society. As a young man he was pushed to learn Sanskrit, the language of Gods. However, memorizing chapters and verses was hard work and he hated to work hard. He learned some but never mastered the language. In later years, he wanted his sons to be scholars and like his own father, he too pushed his sons to study hard. But they had their own way of doing things and studying hard was not one of these. As if to compensate his own shortcomings he wanted a son in law well versed in Sanskrit.

Through friends and relatives and friends of relatives the Pandas scouted young men from their own caste as a prospective son in law. In every instance, all the factors did not match. One of the young men was a good scholar and came from a reasonably aristocratic background. But the young man's father was addicted to hashish and was rumored to have stolen money from a man in his village. Durgesh Panda could not bear the fact that his daughter would be a part of a family whose members had a questionable reputation.

Almost regularly the Pandas kept getting information about a prospective family or a prospective young man. Durgesh Panda followed the lead and visited the family and researched the background. But nothing seemed to be satisfactory.

When Haru became 14 years old and was still living at her parents' house it became a matter of concern. In order to find a good son- in- law the parents did all kinds of Puja and offered all kinds of sacrifices to many Gods and Goddesses they regularly worshipped. Outwardly both Sati Panda and her husband did their day- to -day things. She looked after the smooth running of the household. She took care of the planning of meals and watched over female domestic hands drew water from the well, made cow dung patties, chafed husks from rice, made pastes of lentil by grinding a foot long round stone over a flat stone. Durgesh Panda visited the farmland and supervised his workers. He kept accounts of the inflow and outflow of his money. His sons at times helped him. But behind all their daily and mundane activities the husband and wife shared a sense of worry that was understandable only to the two of them.

Haru, on her part, felt like she was living in limbo. She did not have to prepare for her studies anymore. She was not free to mix or play with others as easily as she used to do as a child. Neither a grown woman nor a child, she felt like she was suspended over a strange horizon. From Paru she was getting all the frustrating information about her parents not being able to find a husband for her. She was aware of all the Pujas taking place in their house recently. Her parents were trying to please the Gods and Goddesses for her. She was ashamed of herself for causing so much worry to her parents.

In her gloomiest moments Haru foresaw dark clouds eclipsing in her future. She imagined herself as a woman without a husband and forever dependent on her parents and brothers. In a mood of utter darkness she wished she were never born. It would have spared her parents a lot of agony and anxiety, she thought. While no one was looking she would weep in silence. By now she had two sisters- in- law. All of them lived in the same house. At times, they teased her about her prospective suitors and their shortcomings. Like Haru, they too had been girls once. And having gone through the process of rejection themselves they seemed to be unconcerned about her fate. So it was impossible for her to share her innermost feelings with them. As newly arrived daughters in law in the Panda household they had very little to say in the decision making. Like all other women in the village they lived like appendages to their husband's existence in the house. Besides, who would contradict Sati Panda? She was the absolute ruler in her household. The daughters in law kept busy cooking all day. They performed all kinds of rituals dictated by their mother- in- law. With perfect obedience they managed their lives under her guidance with full knowledge that one day, someday in the future, they will be on their own and make decisions for themselves.

The household was full of comings and goings all the time. Because of the number of people involved, there was always some sort of commotion inside and outside the Panda household. The brothers had their circle of friends who dropped by now and then. Then the farmhands and their wives and children had always some needs that were to be taken care of. There were visitors who came to see Durgesh Panda who had ever so many ways of dealing with people at all levels. This is how the family seemed to thrive. Haru's impending marriage and attempts to find a husband for her, just added to the ongoing commotion.

The young men of the family – Haru's two brothers – did not have much to say in this matter. As long as their parents were still living, all affairs pertaining to the home life was their responsibility. In matters like this it was the father who made all the decisions and Durgesh Panda was quite capable of making wise decisions about his children. That is how he arranged the marriage of his two sons. The young women who came to his house as daughters- in- law knew how to write their names and could read a hand written letter. But their manners – the way they conducted themselves in their in- law's house – was remarkable. The two young women acted like sisters. There was never a hitch between them. They were respectful toward their mother- in- law and toward him. They helped the household run smoothly. And this is what Durgesh Panda liked the most. He also wanted his older daughter Haru to learn these beautiful qualities of obedience, affection, tolerance, as well as cooking, from her two competent sisters- in- law.

Almost every day Haru spent considerable time in the company of her sisters – in - law. More often than not Paru joined her. But she talked too much and teased her mercilessly. She wondered if Paru was jealous of her for getting all the attention of a future bride. Haru liked her sister's company in spite of its drawbacks. But she enjoyed more being with either of her sisters in law. Each of them knew how to stitch and how to make cakes. By working with them, together or separately, she was able to pick up new tricks. From their way of dealing with her mother she learned the nuances of interaction between a daughter in law and a mother in law. The newly wed young women had no formal responsibility for her. She was not under their charge as long as her parents were alive. But in a very subtle way she picked up ideas and clues from them to use in her future. Often she felt sad in the expectation that one day she would leave their company to go to her own in law's house.

One afternoon Paru came to her sister with a big giggle on her face as if she was going to burst into laughter.

"What is it, Paru?" – asked she

"Nothing" – said Paru but could not stop laughing.

"What is it?" asked Haru again in mock annoyance.

"This is it. This is the end. Now you have to start packing your bag"- said Paru.

Haru could not ask her "why". At the same time she was dying to know the details. Especially the way Paru got to know what she claims to have known. Her silence did the trick. Now Paru began to describe.

"Daddy was telling mother about this guy who is a distant relative of someone. I have never seen him. Daddy says that he is really cute". Paru put a lot of emphasis on the word cute. "He does not have much money. His father died when he was young. So there is only he with his old mother and younger sister."

Haru wanted to hear all the details about "this man" as quickly as possible. Therefore without asking a single question she just kept looking at her sister while Paru continued.

"The way Daddy talks about him, he really likes the guy. His not having money does not bother Daddy because the man knows a lot of Sanskrit. Daddy seems to be sold on him. Oh yes, he hobnobs with a Sadhu who lives in the temple in their village. This guy's mother is afraid that her son may become a Sadhu himself. Therefore, she wants to find a daughter in law very soon."

"Now you must grab this guy before he becomes a holy man" – said Paru in a mischievous way.

"What did mother say?"

"Mother was kind of silent. She was listening without uttering a word and was very quiet. After daddy finished talking, he wanted to know her mind. But she did not say much. "Well if you think the boy is good enough for our Haru then I am with you" This is all she could say. Then I heard her sobbing. All of a sudden she became emotional. I hate when mother does that all the time. Daddy and mother did not know that I was on the other side of the wall"

Haru took a deep breath. Momentarily she became overjoyed and speechless. Her heart quivered and shrank in the fear of an unknown anticipation called married life. For a moment, both sisters looked at each other and at the same time burst out in uncontrolled laughter. Haru had tears of happiness in her eyes. Instantly, she prayed in her mind and asked blessings from all the Gods and Goddesses she knew or remembered.

The sisters were still hugging each other when the younger sister in law – Bhupa's wife – came striding toward them. By now the entire household had come to know about Durgesh Panda's thinking. For everyone in the family it was important news and each of them wanted to get as much mileage as possible from the announcement. The sister- in -law wanted to be the good news bearer for Haru. Looking at the two sisters she said "So you know."

"What," asked Paru

"The big news" said the sister- in- law

"I know nothing about it. " –Paru protested.

The sister- in -law did not fully believe her. But taking both of them aside she gave all the details of what she was given by her mother- in- law by way of information. "Looks like this is going to stick"- was her last comment.

Durgesh Panda had met Harish at a function in a nearby village. The young man came there with a group of people from his village. The way he carried himself in the group attracted Pandababu's attention and he started digging into the younger man's whereabouts.

One of the guests from Harish's village, an older man, struck up a conversation with Durgesh Panda and was very helpful in providing information about the young man. First of all, Harish, of lighter complexion with bright eyes and straight nose, was from the same caste as Panda. Unlike many others of his age he did not chew 'pan' or smoke home made cigarettes. He was thin and straight as a bamboo stick. Harish was unmarried. Durgesh Panda learned that Harish, fatherless since the age 12, had been supporting his mother and sister. Immediately, in a paternal way, he liked the young man. Before Harish left the function Durgesh Panda made it a point to talk to him. In a clever way the older man assessed the behavior and manners of the young man. He was pleased with what he saw: The young man was very polite but not shy. He spoke fluently without pitching his voice too high. He appeared to be respectful of others, especially of older people. The very last quality of him impressed Panda greatly. "This is it" he thought to himself about his search for a son – in - law.

It was obvious that the young man did not have much in the way of material wealth. This did not disturb Panda at all. By just looking at the young man he had drawn the conclusion that God willing if the young man marries Haru then together they can form a strong nest full of prosperity and happiness. On his way home Durgesh Panda could hardly hide his glee about what he had found. He was absolutely sure that the young man's mother would have no objection to taking Haru as her daughter- in- law. After talking to his wife, Durgesh Panda consulted his stars to make his next move.

The process required a few breathing exercises and consulting an astrologer who measured the movement of stars related to his horoscope. Finally an auspicious moment was carved out. On that moment of that day, Durgesh Panda of Soroda went to Harish's village with the proposal for Haru's marriage.

It was not difficult for Pandababu to find the house. Harish was well known in the village. Yet, the older people still called him his father's son. The way people directed a newcomer to the house, he felt that the young man's mother had a commanding presence in her immediate neighborhood. The house was probably one of the smallest in the village. An extended porch on the front was covered with palm leaves. This was used as a living room. There was a large yard around the house. A cow and a calf were tied to a post there.

When Durgesh Panda arrived at the front door of the little house, only Sumi was there. She was about Paru's age. Her brother at the moment was at his school teaching and her mother had just stepped out to do some errands. A stranger's arrival at the house had not gone unnoticed by the neighbors. And it did not take very long for Jhumpi to know that someone was at her door. She returned home as hurriedly as she could.

Durgesh Panda introduced himself to the mistress of the house and after some exchange of pleasantries explained his purpose for coming. He caught Jhumpi off guard. She was not prepared to enter into a marriage related negotiation for her son and needed a few moments to collect her thoughts. She approached the issue this way "Brother, you just arrived under such a hot sun. Have some lunch and take a little rest. We are not leaving the house. We will still be here when you finish resting."

There was sincerity in her voice and Durgesh Panda felt disarmed. He knew that in a situation like this any protestation would not work. So he obliged the hostess.

In the early afternoon, after taking some rest, Durgesh Panda sat across from his hostess and the two approached the issue of the wedding of their offspring. It was a bit awkward for Panda to approach the subject because the negotiator in front of him was a woman.

"Sister, I have come to your house with a big expectation. I hope you won't disappoint me"- said Durgesh Panda.

"Everything is in God's hand- replied his hostess. This was a vague statement. But it served the purpose. She did not commit to anything and at the same time kept all her options open.

"My daughter Haru is a very sweet girl. She is totally unaware of the crookedness of the world. In a small family like yours she would fit in very well. Besides, you have a wonderful son. I am very impressed with his behavior and manners. As a son- in- law he would be an asset to our family. You must be proud of him."

Having heard so many good things about her son from a stranger's mouth Jhumpi felt really proud of her son. Yes, for some time she had been looking for a daughter-in-law. But never in her wildest dreams did she think that Durgesh Panda of Soroda would be at her doorstep with a wedding proposal between his daughter and her son. In order to digest the situation, in her customary way, Jhumpi wanted some time. But Durgesh Panda wanted an answer right away. He wanted to fix the wedding day before he left. In a matter like this she wanted to be cautious, very cautious. First of all, she wanted to know a bit more about her prospective daughter-in law – her behavior, her upbringing, her mother's background. She was confident that given her contacts and skills she would be able to find out all of that within a few days. Secondly, she did not want to give the impression that she was thrilled – even if she actually was – because the girl was a rich man's daughter. As the mother of the groom she wanted to have the upper hand. She wanted Durgesh Panda to come back one more time so that she could show him that in matters relating to her children she was the boss. She knew that if the Pandas really wanted her son they would not mind coming back one more time. That is exactly what happened. In spite of all his skills in bargaining and persuading Pandababu found his hostess to be tough-minded.

She was polite, yet stubborn while "begging" for a few more days to give him a definite answer.

"We are not as well off as you are. When Harish's father was alive we had everything. But now we have become the poorest of the poor. Coming from a rich home like yours, I do not know if your daughter can accept us. Harish is my only son. He is the apple of my eye. All my hopes rest with him. I do not want to see him miserable with an unhappy wife". Tears welled up in her eyes as she said this.

"Haru is very understanding, very modest. I am sure with your love and kindness she would not mind any deprivation. Besides, what is poverty and what is wealth? They are all part of the same grand illusion."

Durgesh Panda was telling this from his own experience. He grew up as a poor boy. But he married well. With the help from his wife's dowry, Panda was able to buy acres of good farmland. Later, he started his moneylending business and the effort was a sure passport to bigger wealth. He enjoyed his wealth. At the same time a belief was ingrained in him that both wealth and poverty were two different sides of the same coin. He was not sure whether the lady in front of him actually understood what he said. So he paraphrased it in a different way:

"Sister, I was once a poor boy. With God's grace I have enough to feed my family now. In the larger scheme of things my wealth does not mean anything." He took a deep breath and then continued his conversation. "Once upon a time you were rich. Now, you are poor. So what? Sooner or later your situation would change. You have a handsome, intelligent son and I want him for my daughter" he concluded.

His voice was persuasive. Just by listening to him Jhumpi could sense that his feelings were genuine. She did not want to disappoint him. At the same time she did not want to appear gong ho. As the mother of the groom, in this particular case, she was determined to have the upper hand.

"Brother, you can't imagine how relieved I feel now. I have

been praying for about a year to find a good girl for my son. Finally, I have found one in your house. Let me do my prayer on your proposal for seven days. If my prayer is answered by the deity then we can proceed according to his will." In a very polite way Jhumpi was bluffing her guest. Since she mentioned her prayer and the deity, no further argument was possible by any one. Durgesh Panda had no choice but agree to come back.

"I will return in nine days to finalize the matter" he said.

"God willing" was the only answer she would give him. That day Harish did not come for his midday meal. By learning of the arrival of Durgesh Panda of Soroda he deliberately stayed away. He was too embarrassed to have a groom seeking visitor in his house.

The following day Jhumpi called one of the women in the village who usually hawked her trinkets by traveling further distances from the village. She asked the woman if she had ever traveled to hawk in Soroda. The woman said that she had. She also told Jhumpi some tidbits about the Panda girls but could not remember which one was the older between the two. Jhumpi asked her if as a favor she would again be willing to go to Soroda to gather some more facts about the prospective bride's family. She offered the woman some rice and promised her more of the same when she returned.

Within two days she had all the information she needed. After talking to the woman for the second time she was convinced that the deity had really answered her prayers.

In Durgesh Panda's house in Soroda, since his conversation with Jhumpi, uncertainty was causing a lot of anxiety. Everyone knew that in the negotiating process anything could go wrong. Having learned more from her husband about Harish, Sati Panda had become enthusiastic about the young man. But his mother seemed to throw a monkey wrench on her hope and enthusiasm. In her silent prayer Sati Panda asked for everything to go well for her daughter and prayed for her prospective mother-in-law's change of heart. For Sati Panda, at this moment , the other woman was a villain.

On his part, Durgesh Panda was convinced that everything would go well and saw no reason to the contrary. However, he did not like the way he was put off by Harish's mother." Well, marriage is a complicated thing," he assured himself.

Haru who was getting all the information through her younger sister was afraid to see another proposal fail. She had built up her hope and did not want it dashed once again. A sense of anxiety took over her body and soul. She lost her appetite. "Is prayer an answer?" she asked herself. But there was no reply. She felt helpless. For several days, everyone in the Panda household seemed to be on pins and needles. They wanted things to end on a positive note.

On the ninth day, as promised, Durgesh Panda and a couple of his relatives arrived at Jhumpi's doorstep. By then she was ready and knew that they would come. Therefore, she had instructed Sumi on that day to pay special attention to her curries. She herself had taken in charge of cooking. From her side, Jhumpi had invited a few relatives from the village to join the guests.

When the visitors from Soroda broached the issue of their daughter's wedding, Jhumpi told Pandababu that the deity did answer her prayer and according to his instruction her daughter-in-law lived in Pandababu's house. Such a revelation by Jhumpi overjoyed her guests. According to the custom, a celebratory feast took place in her house. The wedding date was fixed. All the details such as when the groom would arrive in Soroda, how many people would come with him, what kind of food and haw many courses should be served to the groom's party - were decided by the people gathered. When it came to the question of dowry, everyone had to abide by Jhumpi's rule. She was the guardian of the house. She did not want any discussion of that subject. She had her own reasons for this.

She knew that Durgesh Panda was a wealthy man and would not let his daughter go to her in-law's house without any gold ornament or cash. She did not want others to know all the details about her transaction. Secondly, she had a very small house that had no room for a whole lot of new things such as furniture, clothes or a wooden chest.

A wedding in the village was not just between a young man and a young woman. It was also the bonding between two families of both the bride and the groom. Wedding was not a momentary thing. It was a process that lasted several days. Finally, at an auspicious moment of an auspicious day Harish and Haru were pronounced man and wife. According to the custom, a holy fire was witness to their eternal vow. There were continuous feasts at the Panda house. All the guests were treated properly. And the wedding was complete without a hitch. The family observed all the rituals required for a daughter's wedding.

After the wedding, Haru left her parent's house with her husband. The moment for which she had waited for so long with so much of anticipation arrived suddenly and she was jolted by its impact. She wore rings on her fingers and a gold necklace around her slender neck. For the first time, she had a red dot on her forehead at the parting of her hair. This was the symbol that she was a married woman now.

3

In her husband's house Haru found herself in a totally unfamiliar surrounding. She did not know her inlaws at all and had never seen them before. She even did not know who Harish was until Paru told her about him. Once she came to their house, all of them became her own people now. They acted as if she had been a part of their lives forever. The expression of affection that came her way made her comfortable. She was genuinely thankful about it. However, there were some practical things that at the beginning she found a bit hard to handle.

She had to draw water from a well that was dug deep about 30 feet below the ground and was about 6 feet wide. There was an earthen fence around this huge hole. Leaning against the fence she had to tie a rope around a jug or a bucket to draw water from the well. Every time Haru looked at the depth of the well she felt like her head was reeling. After a few times of practice she got used to it.

Unlike her parent's house the house she came into was very small and there was hardly enough space for four people to move around. During the wedding, a handful of relatives seemed to have camped in and around the house. The little house became like a packed sardine can. Eventually, one by one, the relatives left. And now she was able to move around the house. Her mother-in- law was hardly ever inside. She was always outside doing something - either taking care of the cow or collecting firewood or getting some errands done. She did not seem to have a whole lot of physical strength. For her age she looked much older and frail. Haru sometimes felt sorry for her mother in law who always seemed to be working too hard. She had never, ever seen her mother back home working that way.

Harish was the sole provider for the family. His income from his teaching job was hardly adequate for the food and clothing for every one. Whatever her mother in law made from her milk products supplemented the family's income. Therefore, the cow was an integral and important part of the family. There was always some type of shortage in the house which no one in the family seemed to mind. They had been accustomed to living without many things. What felt like a shortage to Haru no one in her new house seemed to bother about.

Haru learned to live frugally. She had to. As a new daughter in law in the house she felt responsible to take charge of the family's budget. For her, adding or subtracting was not such a big job. She realized that the important thing she had to do was juggling the various needs and prioritizing each one of them. In spite of her juggling and rearranging the priorities in her mind, the reality of the financial difficulties did not go away. She started ignoring them more and more. She learned to make cakes without sugar. She made fries without much oil. At her parents' house she used to throw away partially spoiled fruits and vegetables. In her new house she learned to salvage the unspoiled portions of fruits and vegetables and made good use of them.

For a long time Harish and his mother and sister had been

living without many ordinary things that others took for granted. They lived frugally. And their needs seemed to be dictated by what was available to them and it was not much. All their needs were basic. Enough food, straw for the roof, and new clothes for Sumi during Diwali – these were the things that Harish and his mother seemed to worry about. As time went by Haru became accustomed to their way of thinking. She forgot the way she used to live at her parents' house and eventually it became a distant past. Like sugar losing itself in water she became an integral part of her new household where unlike her parent's house the shortage of material things ruled the day. Yet, she saw no reason to complain. To whom was she going to complain, anyway? Why? Her husband was trying his best. Her mother in law was always busy. The fact that there was not enough to go around was a situation that was beyond the control of any one of them. Having been married to Harish she had cast her lot with him and as his wife she was determined to endure with him whatever came her way – shortages included.

Whenever hawkers came to the neighborhood, she always avoided them. A new daughter in law is supposed to buy trinkets for her kitchen and for her new wardrobe. Haru avoided such luxury. She knew if she bought a new comb or a new scarf or a bottle of hair oil she had to take money from other things. She could not do that. Over time she devised ways to avoid hawkers by saying "Mother in law has the key to the chest. And I don't know when she would be back "or "It is Thursday. We are not supposed to part with coins today" – were her favorite explanations. She managed to say these things so convincingly that they actually believed what she said.

Everyone knew that Haru came from a rich family. It was a common assumption among women in the village that her parents gave her a lot of gold and silver ornaments in marriage and that Haru had money. They universally thought that Harish was lucky to have such a beautiful wife. For the women of the neighborhood Haru appeared to be very unassuming. There was not a trace of pretentiousness in her. Unlike other women in the village she knew how to read and write. Therefore, she kind of mystified them.

Haru's most ardent admirer was her mother in law. She was impressed with all the ornaments, jewelry and clothes Haru had brought with her. Jhumpi thought that all the clothes, sweets, gold, silver and other nice things that Haru brought to her house were befitting for a princess. She wanted no one to know about her new wealth. It was none of their business. She wanted the neighbors to keep guessing. Jhumpi knew that almost every woman in the neighborhood was nosy about the newcomer. They wanted to see her ornaments. They wanted to know about her parents and friends. Above all else they wanted to taste her cooking. She had to protect Haru from all the nosy women of the neighborhood.

Nobody knew more than Jhumpi about poverty and misfortune. At the beginning she was not sure about how much the young woman would accept her new home with all its problems and shortcomings. But Haru did not have any problem in fitting into her family. Not even once did she mention how privileged and pampered she used to be at her parent's house. She took care of the cooking and cleaning. She woke up in the morning before anyone else did. She was careful about what she talked about and whom she talked to.

Haru was not secretive about describing her parents or her childhood. But she did not brag about them. In her description she was truthful but modest. A lot of things she deliberately omitted about herself and her family at her parent's house. Therefore, the information she gave out was bare bones and could not be used in a derogatory way. Talking to the women in the neighborhood was like maneuvering through a minefield. In their heart of their hearts they were looking for something to gossip about. Haru showed a great deal of skill and nerve to outwit them and they did not even know it.

Jhumpi found her daughter in law to be a hard working, smart and unpretentious young lady with a strong sense of compassion. In spite of all the shortages in the world that she faced in her own house, Haru never let a beggar go away empty handed from her door. Before she sat down to eat the young lady made sure that the cows ate and drank well. Jhumpi never had time to take a nap in the afternoon. Lately, with the prodding of her daughter in law she had to try to take a nap in the middle of the day

"Ma, you should not work all the time. You look tired. You should rest when the sun is so hot" she would say.

"Who is going to do my job if I take a nap?" Jhumpi would reply in mock anger.

"Ma, you have been working hard all of your life. I can do some of your work. That is why I am here." Such matter of fact expression from Haru would disarm her. Just to obey Haru's request - hot sun or not - she would try in vain to take a nap in the middle of the day. Small things like these are not earth shattering qualities. But they were important for a young lady to establish good credentials with her in laws. Jhumpi was pleased to find such a wife for her son. At the same time she was very pleased to have such a good role model for her daughter Sumi whose marriage, in her motherly thoughts, was not too far away.

Harish was totally attracted toward Haru because in its own way her voice was the most soothing he had ever heard.

Since Haru came into his life, Harish's stature in the village took an upward turn. Now that he was a married man he seemed to command more respect. Older people seemed to pay more attention. This was a new experience for him. Up until now, he was looking up to his mother for advice in the matter of running the house. His opinion did not count. All that changed after Haru's arrival. She always wanted his opinion and ideas and it made him feel important. He liked to eat good food like fish curry, fried rice, banana pancakes, samosha and dosha. She prepared those dishes well. Haru's expertise in cooking was amazing. "You give her a handful of green grass and she can make the most delicious pancake out of it" he thought.

Harish knew that there were a handful of dishes that no one in the world could make as good as his mother did. But on a day-to- day basis, Haru's delicious cooking topped the chart. When he let her know how impressed he was with her skills, she would coyly look the other way or move away with a shy smile. She did not want to be compared with other people - definitely, not with her mother in law.

Haru had read a noticeable amount of the literatures produced in her language called Odia. She had read about stories and incidents that other women in the village – young or old – would not know. Her knowledge of Odia also had led her to learn some Sanskrit, the root of many Indian languages. She had memorized quite a few devotional songs. In a way she was somebody with whom Harish now could discuss matters other than mundane things like grazing the cow or digging a hole in the backyard. With his mother, a discussion of anything was out of the question. She was always wrapped up in her own world. She had set ideas about everything. Either you agreed with her or she went her own way. But with Haru the situation was different. Haru always gave importance to the views of others. Even if she were right she would not press her opinion on anybody. She would go along and accommodate. This was a quality that easily disarmed a strong willed person including his mother.

There was something about Haru that Harish found irresistible but could not pinpoint exactly what it was. He longed for her company. He felt lonely when he was away from her. The way she looked at him, the way she talked to him, the way she involved herself in the day to day affairs of the house, the way she treated his mother and sister and the way she accepted her new environment seemed amazing to Harish. All of these qualities were a part of" Haru's charm" that was so alluring and so irresistible to him. Like a bee to the flower he seemed to be more attracted and drawn to her with every passing day. However, at the beginning the situation had been different.

For Harish, Haru was a stranger. She arrived in his house as a new bride. He had never seen her before. Now, she came into his life as his wife. But he did not have the foggiest idea about how the relationship between a man and his wife works. He had seen and heard all his life about people getting married and living under the same roof in the same house and having children and getting old together. But he was clueless about how all this related to his own situation.

According to the ritual in order to be in the same room with his new wife he had to wait four more days after the wedding. Finally after four days the time came and Haru was led by one of his older cousins to their bedroom. There was a lamp burning in the corner of the room. That night in their bedroom he saw Haru's face in the flickering light of a dim oil lamp. Haru looked very shy.

By then, all the rituals of the wedding had been finished. There were still guests in the house. The relatives seemed to swarm in the little place. Harish was anxious. Both Haru and he seemed to be unsure of their presence in the same room. Like a frozen statue, Haru stood silently in the room by the bed. To Harish it felt like an eternity. He did not know what to say to her.

" You should not stand like that" she told Harish in a very low voice.

She continued to remain frozen. Then he came up to her and guided her to the bed. She seemed to be hesitant. Her hand in his, she walked very slowly up to the bed with him. She had a feeling as if her body was going to give in and she was going to collapse. She was very nervous. Neither of them seemed to know what to say to each other and how to act. Nothing in life had prepared them for the moment at hand.

Up to that point, Harish had this idea ingrained in his mind that a man's marriage brings his downfall as he becomes sidetracked from his original goal. Ideally speaking, a man should seek salvation by renouncing the temptations of the world. And a woman for a man was a temptation. Freedom from marriage kept him free to serve people as well as the will of his Creator. He admired the Sadhu because of his bravery to do all of these things.

In the present situation Harish got married so that his mother would not be upset. As her only son he felt obligated to carry out her will. Yet, the desire to resist temptation in life was still very strong in him. So that night, in spite of Haru's presence in his life, he did not want to lose his religious seeking. There was no kissing between them. And he did not come close to his new bride. He held her hand. It felt soft and sweaty. In the flickering light of the lamp he saw her beautiful black eyes. He touched her long black hair. On the one hand he felt totally inhibited by the presence of so many people just outside their bedroom wall. On the other hand he wanted to be a Brahmachari, a celibate while still married to Haru. That night, while holding Haru's hand and enjoying it at the same time he fell asleep.

Haru did not know what her role was in this situation. No one at home had openly discussed this subject with her. She had not asked about her mother or sisters- in- law. She had read Kamasutra before her wedding and was aware of Mudras or different positions of love making. But they were all academic. About the actual thing, the real exercise, she had no idea. When Harish escorted her to their bed it gave her a new sensation – a kind of sensation she had never felt before. She was hesitant, ambivalent and anxious. Her heart pounded like a drum. At the same time she was very happy to be married and very happy to be with her husband. Since she had no idea about how a newlywed couple behaves with each other on their first night together, she did not sense any abnormality in Harish's behavior. For her it was neither withdrawal nor resistance. She just accepted it as a very normal male behavior on her husband's part. Haru had no idea about her husband's inner conflicts. At the moment, the only thing that she could feel was her husband's hand. His touch was very soothing.

For a long while after her husband fell asleep she stayed awake and stayed seated on the bed. No particular thing was going through her head. It was strange for her to hear a man breathe next to her. But she enjoyed the vibration of his breathing in that little room. After some time, in the middle of the night, the wicker of the oil lamp burned out. The room became engulfed with complete darkness. She finally dosed off.

A newlywed young woman was not supposed to stay in bed after daybreak. It did no good to her reputation to be a late riser. As soon as the horizon lit up, the crows crowed, the birds chirped and all kinds of activities started taking place. As soon as the sun rose in the sky, the village - full of chaos and promises - came to its full life. It would have been difficult for Haru to lie awake and hear all that noise from nearby trees. She woke up at daybreak and left the bed. In the cool breeze of the early morning she drew a bucket of water from the well, washed her face and did some familiar chores before anyone in the house woke up. Her mother in law was very pleased to see her rise so early in the morning.

Jhumpi treated her daughter in law like her own daughter. She knew that no matter what she did or said she could never become Haru's mother. But Haru was her son's wife who in future would bear her grandchildren. Therefore, she was as good as a daughter or even more.

Haru's willingness to work hard and her habit of paying attention to little things won over everybody and this impressed her mother in law a great deal. As a girl Haru did not have to do many of the household jobs. There were others for that. But here at her new home she had to do them herself. Even if some of that work at the beginning was awkward she mastered them by practice. "Well, I did not know how to draw water from the well. So it was naturally difficult" she consoled herself.

Like all the newly married women in the village she was confined to her in law's house. This was the tradition. Cooking, cleaning, housework – these were the things that she was supposed to do and she did them diligently. In the mornings she left her bed before anybody else. In the night she went to bed after attending to all the work that needed to be done. Usually, after sunset there was very little action anywhere in the village. The fire flies roamed in the darkness, Crickets made sounds, the frogs in the pond croaked at night. As far as activities went, there were none.

At times, after completing her evening's cooking, she sat near her stove. Sumi and Jhumpi joined her. They engaged in small talk. Whose daughter is getting married where, whose son went to work in Calcutta, whose cow gave birth to a heifer, who grows the best quality of melon in the village, what spice is the most appropriate for which curry – were the kinds of things they talked about. Every night Jhumpi would sit down around the stove and among other conversations she would uncork a small part of her life story. Her own mother in law's behavior toward her when she came to this house as a young bride, how she grew up in her parents' house, what kind of clothes she used to wear, her husband's death and its circumstances, how the neighbors treated her after her husband died, which neighbor was helpful and which one was not – she narrated in detail and bit by bit Haru came to know about the older woman's past. The mother in law also told her about the harrowing flood their area experienced about 30 years ago. She mentioned the fire that burned down the entire village of her parents when she was a little girl. No matter how much she narrated, Haru felt that there were still more stories to come. From her mother in law she learned something about her neighbors and the village in which they lived. .

Jhumpi told her daughter in law many tales of sorrow and happiness. She offered the young woman examples and speculations and hypothesis. But Jhumpi's stories always started with a fact followed by her personal spin. For her, they were real. Jhumpi narrated to her the stories that happened half a century ago or just last year. At times Haru was awed by the things her mother in law said she had gone through. With her limited experience as a daughter in law she could only imagine them. At times she wished that some of those things would never happen to her or to anyone else. But they were distant and at times unfamiliar to Haru. Most of the names and incidents Jhumpi mentioned were unknown to her. Given the lack of personal experience about many things Haru could only try to imagine them. Yet, she could not picture everything clearly in her mind. She listened to the stories attentively out of curiosity. With all those stories and experiences tied to her life, Jhumpi appeared in her eyes a figure that was mystical and remote.

One particular night, after long talks among the women of the house, Jhumpi fell asleep by the stove side. It was a night of full moon. Their front door was still open. And the reflection of the moon made the surroundings look bright. There was a Jasmine tree full of blooms outside. Its fragrance in the cool breeze wafted into the house. Even if it mixed with the smell of the cow dung fire and mustard oil cooking, the jasmine still retained its identity. The moonlight, the evening breeze and the sweet smell of jasmine made Haru very happy. This was a kind of happiness she had never felt before.

In spite of all the work she had done all day she was not as tired as others. The stories her mother in law talked about tonight and the moon above made her even more awake. Sumi locked the front door. After the mother and daughter retired to their beds Haru proceeded straight into her bedroom. Other nights, when she entered the room Harish would usually be lying on his side. Tonight he was fully awake and lying on his back. At some point he had managed to light the lamp. So when Haru entered the room her eyes met his. There was a kind of mischief in them.

She had never seen such mischief.

As soon as she set foot in the room, he got off the bed and escorted her to the bed. But tonight was different. He seemed to be much surer of himself and his grip was tighter.

That night, for the first time Harish took his wife's face into his cupped hands and looked straight into her eyes and kissed her. It was warm and there was a kind of wildness about it. Without a word they looked into each other's eyes. Instantly, she collapsed into his arms. They held on to each other tightly. She became so happy in his arms that she almost wept. As if this was the moment for which she had been waiting all her life and the moment was finally at hand.

By then, Harish had given up all his desire to become a Sadhu. This seemed to him like total foolishness – at least at this point in his life. For days he had been thinking about his situation. There seemed to be no solution to his doubts. His Sanskrit verses in different Sastras admired the life of a Sadhu who renounced everything including a sex life. At the same time the verses also advised people to enjoy a healthy family life.

"Which way do I go?" he kept asking himself repeatedly. There seemed to be no clear answer. Finding himself in a jumble of confusion he was forced to take a stand. And he finally did.

Haru's beauty and simplicity were alluring. At times, even while mulling through his doubts, he had thought it to be foolish to lie down next to her and not take advantage of her presence. After all, she was his wife now. And she was such fun to be with! However, he was willing to test his stamina in a strange way.

That night it was a full moon and he was feeling poetic. While the women of the house were talking by the stove, he was tossing and turning in his bed and waiting for Haru's footsteps. He wished their conversation would end. He could hear his mother repeating the same old stories that he had heard about a million and one times. In the past, he enjoyed her stories. But at this moment it seemed to him boring. Finally, when the conversation ended he felt relieved. His mother went to bed. He could hear Sumi closing the door. And finally when Haru with her shy and reluctant footsteps came into their bedroom he was ready to greet her as her husband. He was ready to show her his love. He wanted to tell her how much he loved her. But at the moment, words did not come to him. He seemed to be speechless. He just wanted to look at his wife and wanted to feel her with wild passion. For the first time that night with full display of emotion he made love to her. For the first time in her life Haru realized a sense of fulfillment that made her cry. Very sweetly and repeatedly she told him "I love you"

4

Haru's ability to read and write did not get lost among the women of the village. Like Jhumpi, they also became her admirers. The women were rather thankful that they could now come to someone without inhibition to relate their messages in writing. They took it for granted that reading and writing was for someone special. None of them thought to belong to that category. As far as they were concerned, neither reading nor writing was an indispensable thing for them. So they lived their lives in their usual way without ever feeling guilty.

In the village, life was hard. For the women it was harder. The men folk worked outside in the field. But the women were stuck with all the mundane problems of running the household. They had to cook and clean and take care of the children. In order to please the gods and goddesses they had to do the fasting for the occasion. One practical reason for this fasting was that it saved the family some food that at times seemed to be precious.

A woman was more or less treated like a man's property. If the husband was abusive a woman could not do anything about it. Whatever went wrong in the house it was always her fault. Among the women who endured the most were the newly married daughters in law. It was expected of them to bear a male child within a year or two of their marriage. A male child in the future would grow up to be a man and would perpetuate the family's name. So it was important to have a male child. If a girl was born then the family felt overwhelmed because of the worry that the newborn baby would cost a lot when she gets married twelve or fourteen years later.

Everyone knew that the children are born when a man and a woman get together. But the way the villagers thought, it was the misdeeds of the woman in her previous life that determined whether or not she would have a son. If she did not bear a son then they blamed her previous life. The young woman's mother-in- law constantly reminded her of that. She was told so often and so convincingly that she believed it. Enduring harassment at the hands of the in- laws was taken for granted. And young women silently suffered. Families where all the brothers and their wives and children and all the uncles and aunts lived under the same roof were called a "joint family". Separation among brothers was looked down upon as a bad thing. If a brother wanted to establish a separate household by breaking away from the joint family then it was his wife who got the blame. Everyone thought that it was she who put the idea of separation in his head. Or the woman could not get along with others, so she wanted a household of her own. Things became really ugly at times of family discords. All kinds of abuse and insults were thrown at the other person's wife.

For generations a pattern was established in the life of the village. A young woman goes through all kinds of torment and eventually grows old. She becomes a mother- in -law and treats her daughter – in – law the same way she was treated. The process continues all over again. No one seemed to see any incongruity in it. Since fate always determined everything they did, they saw no way to get out of it. Their endurance became a part of their existence.

By sheer luck, Haru was spared such difficulties. First of all, her mother in law Jhumpi thought it was Harish's good luck that brought both Haru and him together. Haru was educated and was the daughter of a rich father. This gave her special status in Jhumpi's eyes. Besides, Harish was her only son. She loved him dearly and in her own way pampered him. Her love for her son also reflected on his wife. So the relationship between Haru and her mother in law was like that of a mother and daughter. Haru always deferred to the older woman. She sought her opinion on everything. Unlike many other families in the village there was no conflict between them. Many young women, blessed or burdened with a husband, wished they were as lucky as Haru.

The women of the village seemed to be always busy mending their little worlds. They had very little awareness about what was happening outside their immediate surroundings. Yet, the world was changing. A lot of thinking people around the country were trying to make the women of the villages educated – at least make them able to read a handwritten letter. The village was a part of the big picture. One of the people who supported women's education was the Sadhu who spent most of his time in the village temple. He had no family and no children. He did not have to worry about other people's reaction to his thinking. As a Sadhu he was committed to doing well for others. At least that is what he was supposed to do. The Sadhu seemed to be in a strategic situation to tell people about things as they were. Because he represented religion, the people of the village – young and old – respected him. He did not live his life like everyone else in the village. People thought of him as "different". Therefore, at times he was not taken seriously. At times the men would shrug him off and say "Oh, yes. You can say things like that because you are a sadhu and you don't have to worry about anybody other than yourself. You are different". The Sadhu would laugh it off.

In his own mind, the sadhu often realized that the villagers had a lot of old ideas. In the ancient times those ideas might have worked well. But for the present, they seemed to be useless. Yet, every one in the village was so much stuck in the past that collectively they had no desire to move. They were content to be in their present situation. The Sadhu found it to be difficult and disheartening. When some others from outside talked about women's education in every village he became one of the enthusiastic supporters of their idea. He had no plan about how to start the process in the village where he lived. But he was hopeful that a noble thought would eventually find its supporters. He himself could not teach the women in the village. It would be immodest for them to come to see a man. Besides, the temple was not the place where this kind of thing took place. It was at the far end of the village. And for the women, the learning center had to be inside the village. There was no public place for them to congregate.

While the Sadhu was thinking about women's education in the village, Haru's arrival there gave him hope. Before she came as a daughter in law, the sadhu through Jhumpi had known about her. It pleased him a great deal that at least there would be one woman in the village who could read and write. Maybe through her, others could learn to read and write.

The Sadhu kept his thoughts to himself. He knew that a newly wedded woman does not jump into things at her in law's house right away. She needs time. She needs to be familiar with her neighbors, know her surroundings and be comfortable with her in laws.

After some time, the Sadhu discussed the issue of women's education with some important men in the village. They were important because of their age and status. Some agreed with him. Some did not. The difficulty was that there were a whole lot of men in the village who could not read or write. The older men thought it was more important for the men than their wives to learn the alphabet. The women did not have to go outside their immediate surroundings. Men had to go to the market, read the deeds to their lands and sign paper for loans etc. These problems had been lurking under the surface and all of a sudden came out. All of a sudden the priority became teaching the men folk rather than the women of the village.

The Sadhu was a religious man. His religious commitments did not allow him to be tied down to one program or one place. He kept on moving from village to village. The idea of teaching the men folk appealed to him. He was all for it. Yet, he wanted someone else to do the actual job. After much thinking and brainstorming with others he came upon Harish. In him, the Sadhu found a good man who had a commitment to teaching. By working among the children of the village, Harish by then had established a reputation as a good teacher. So every one thought he could be good for the older people also. Besides, the entire village seemed to like him.

Finally, they set a date for the school to start in the evening. After the day's work the illiterate men gathered under hurricane lamps to learn there ABCs. On that particular occasion, a small celebration took place with participants sharing tea and pastries. And then the real work began.

On the first evening, only a handful of men showed up. But by the end of the week there were twice as many. Their enthusiasm compensated for their lack of brilliance. They continued to stumble on spelling, addition and subtraction. Occasionally, one or two would fall asleep while staring at the alphabets or numbers written on their slates. Others would help wake them up. The sleepers would be embarrassed. But they could not help themselves. A hard day's work made them tired. They would try not to fall asleep again. Eventually, each participant in the evening school learned to sign his name, read a book and was able to compose an application. Most of them learned to write letters with their own thoughts. There were not too many books to go around. Most of them could not afford to buy a book. Paper was costly. So they learned to write on a slate. The men shared their books with each other. In addition to all the pujas and fairs that took place in the village this new effort in the form of an evening school expressed the collective will of the village.

Because of their ability to read and write, the men also became interested in songs and music. Now they could read the poems and songs of their favorite authors. They could recite popular songs of ancient poets. If one of them started singing a song, the entire student body would join him. The cacophony of off key renditions did not bother them a bit. It was a matter of pride for each of them that they were able to read and write and sing a song from the book.

The students in many cases were breadwinners for their families. They grew grains, harvested vegetables and sold their products. Harish did not charge them anything for his work. He did not have to. With gratitude, the students offered him several pounds of rice at the end of the month. No money changed hands.

Once the evening school for men took hold in the village, the Sadhu broached the idea of teaching the women. At this point he did not face any resistance. Many men were willing to let their wives, daughters and daughters in law learn to read and write. However, some of the older people thought that education for women was useless because the women stayed home. Therefore, they did not need any education. Since neither they nor their sons knew anything about the alphabet they were not willing to allow their daughters- in- law to be "educated". A smart woman talks back to her in- laws" was their profound fear and they wanted to discourage such possibilities.

Gently persuaded by the Sadhu, a handful of families finally agreed to allow their daughters in law to learn the alphabet. They did so out of curiosity mixed with respect for him. They knew that he meant well and was a religious man. His persuasiveness still could not dispel their deep-rooted conviction that a woman did not need to learn to read.She needed devotion not smartness.

It was understood that Haru was going to teach the women in her own house. She was the only woman in the village who knew how to read and write. The in- laws seemed to be comfortable with the thought that she was a fresh, innocent face in the village. Therefore, she could not influence others with any bad qualities or ideas.

With blessings from elders in the village who finally allowed women to be educated, Haru started her class on a sunny afternoon in February. Four women showed up on the first day. The following day there were five. By the end of the month there were ten. At the beginning the women came to the class wearing their finest clothes and jewelry. For them it was a chance to get out of the house. As they felt comfortable with their surroundings for learning, their need to be comfortable rather than classy increased and they began to come wearing less formal attire.

Since women were the cooks in their houses each of them wanted to show her best in cooking. Everyday before the class there would be an informal snack. The women would taste each other's rice cake or fried dough or freshly made flakes. There would be green chili, sea salt and onion to spice up their snack. Snack time was also an informal time to catch up with necessary gossip. Above all else, getting together for learning made those women happy. Some of them had never held a slate or a pencil in their hands. They were grown women with all kinds of commitments to their children, their husbands and in-laws.

At home, they had left unwashed clothes. Cows waited for them to be fed. They had to dry cow dung patties when they returned home. Peeling husks from rice paddies depended on them. If one of their children was sick, they worried to death. Given these never-ending worries, each woman seemed to carry a heavy load on her mind. By talking to each other they lessened the weight of the load. Yet, its presence in the mind was a reason for distraction. Some of the women did not do well in learning to read. Some stumbled in learning their addition and division. But none of them gave up. They tried repeatedly. One of Haru's students was her sister in law Sumi. She liked reading and writing

They tried to memorize words and sentences even if the meanings were not clear to them. The women did not have to take an exam. They had no need for it. They were free to drop out at any time. But they did not. At times, their coming to learn also was being used to ridicule them at home. If one of Haru's students said something disagreeable at home, her husband or in laws would say "Oh, she is talking too smart because now she can write her name."

Haru was much younger than a few of them. In their culture, one's age was a very important factor in determining one's place. While teaching reading or multiplication Haru was respectful to them and they learned from her with affection.

For her salary, the women regularly brought grains, lentils, coconuts and bananas. They brought to their teacher seasonal fruits and vegetables such as mangoes, guavas, eggplants, chili peppers, jack fruits, oranges, sweet potatoes, berries and greens – whatever they grew in their fields or backyards. As a result of their contribution Jhumpi's house always remained filled with all kind of edibles. At times she was even able to sell some of her stuff for cash. Harish was proud of his wife's earning power. No one's wife in the village had ever done such a thing. Haru herself was pleased for being able to get a few pennies. Doing something instead of sitting idle at home gave her satisfaction. In a very practical way she helped her husband. Their combined earning made them relatively affluent. Unlike many in the village they had plenty of food to eat and give away.

One day, while holding her hand Harish asked "Haru, you are working too hard."

"You have been working day and night" replied Haru.

"A man is supposed to work hard." Before he could finish Haru snatched words from his mouth and said "and a woman is supposed to sit on her butt and watch the world go by". They laughed.

The sun was setting in the west. That part of the sky seemed to be filled with primrose and crimson colors. The rays of the setting sun reflected on Haru's cheeks. Harish embraced his wife tightly and kissed her. This was a wild and spontaneous reaction as if his feelings toward Haru burst loose at that moment.

What would Ma think if she saw us like this?" Pleased and embarrassed, Haru gently released herself from his grip and went inside.

That night in bed Harish asked her "Haru, you came to this poor family. I don't have too much materially. Hope you don't regret marrying me"

"Regrets? Why? I have you. That is all the wealth I need" spoke Haru resting her head, full of long black hair, on Harish's shoulder. Drops of warm tears rolled down from her eyes. Harish felt a strong emotion for her. He kissed her in the lips and made love to her.

While Harish and Haru were busy working toward bettering their lives in a loving way , Jhumpi was becoming restless about her daughter's wedding. Sumi was not a little girl anymore. Now it was Harish's responsibility to see that his younger sister got married. She felt that Harish was not searching hard enough to find a husband for his sister. In a mild but persuasive way she let her son know that. It never occurred to her that a girl could find her own husband or choose her own partner in life. Everything in the village rested on many conventions. And these conventions – no matter how ridiculous they may seem to an outsider - were never to be broken. Therefore, Sumi's wedding rested on her brother's shoulder because he was the head of the family now.

A wedding meant feasts, presents and pujas. All this cost money. Harish felt that right now he did not have all the money he needed. Then he also knew that Sumi's marriage must be done. This put him in a no-win situation. He talked to Haru about it. Haru seemed to side with her mother in law. "Well, Sumi's wedding cannot wait just because you don't have money" – said she.

"Where am I going to find money to do all that?" – Harish replied.

"Where there is a will there is a way."

Harish had heard this expression many times before. Right now it did not make any sense to him. It was only a cliché. In a serious moment like this, such a cliché seemed to be useless. For the moment in his eyes Haru appeared to be naïve and impractical.

"You know, the Mishras of Tarapur are interested in Sumi. They are looking for a bride for their middle son. They have three sons. Mrs Mishra saw Sumi somewhere in a fair and was impressed with her. Now she wants Sumi as her daughter in law. I have not been able to give the Mishras any reply.

"Does Ma know about it?"

"I told her. She knows the Mishras. They are our distant relatives. She thinks of Mrs. Mishra highly."

"Are they asking for a dowry?"

"They have not asked for any. But…"

"I know" Haru snatched the word from his mouth. "Don't worry. Things will work out." It was reassuring for Harish to hear those words from his wife. It gave him strength.

The following morning, Haru told her husband to go ahead with the negotiation with the Mishras. She told him that he could sell some of her ornaments to raise cash. The feast was not a problem because they had all the things they needed to feed the neighbors and guests at the wedding. Her mother- in- law also had given her some cash from the sale of the cow dung patties. She had saved the money carefully. Harish did a quick math in his mind and found that all the resources put together were enough to handle the expenses. He felt relieved

Within days the arrangements for Sumi's wedding went full swing. On the occasion of her daughter's wedding, Jhumpi tried her best to calm her nerves. She was happy that her daughter was getting married. And at the same time she was sad to lose her. Sumi had been a part of her life ever since she conceived her. Over and over Jhumpi kept telling herself "I wish her father were alive today. He would be very happy."

On her part, Sumi looked angelic in her new clothes and

ornaments. She went through all the rituals that a bride was supposed to go through. Finally, through all the feasts, pujas and Vedic chanting the ceremony of a Hindu wedding was over and Sumi became a married woman. Then she was ready to be sent to her in laws.

The Mishras were good people. Mr. Mishra, her father in law, assured Jhumpi repeatedly that he and his wife would treat Sumi like their daughter. This was reassuring to everyone. Sumi's husband Raju appeared to be a healthy and good- natured young man who managed the family's farming. It was important to every one on Sumi's side of the family that her inlaws belonged to a well to do family. Before leaving for her in laws Sumi took every one's blessing. Her departure from her parental house was a final break with her childhood. All the women of the village – the girls she played with and the women with whom she learned reading and writing - seemed to gather there to see her off. In the life of the village, incidents like this had happened many times before. Now it was Sumi's turn. Everyone was happy to see her married and everyone wished her good luck.

Even if Sumi's departure from her parental home was a natural progression of things, after the wedding, everyone in the house seemed to miss her. Jhumpi missed her the most. Up until Haru's arrival, there were only three in the family Harish, Sumi and their mother. Harish and Sumi were very close. When he bade her good bye, tears welled up in Harish's eyes. For Haru she was like a replacement of Paru. Their relationship was friendly and affectionate. Haru tried to teach her not only reading and writing but things that a newlywed needs to know. She was fun to be around. Every one missed her presence. It took sometime before life got back to normal in Haru's house. She was happy that her sister- in- law was married now.

5

Within a month of Sumi's wedding the news came from the Pandas that they had found a bridegroom for Paru. So Haru for the first time after four years had to go to her parent's house for a few days to attend her sister's wedding. Her father and brothers had been visiting her regularly. But for her, as a married daughter, returning to the parent's house required a special occasion. Such an occasion was now – the wedding of her younger sister. One of her brothers came and picked her up a few days before the wedding. Harish joined his wife and the in laws on the day of wedding.

Paru in her wedding clothes looked beautiful. The Pandas had made all of the arrangements for the accommodations for the wedding party. As usual, there were feasts, comings and goings of guests, giving and receiving presents and dowries for the groom. The occasion was very festive and celebratory. However, based on his own experience, Harish felt that Paru's wedding was not celebrated in the Panda house in as grand a scale as his and Haru's was. It made him feel important. By the time the wedding was over and the bride left for her in law's house, everyone in the Panda family seemed exhausted.

By leaving Jhumpi home by herself Haru felt that her mother in law was stuck with all the work of the house. It made her feel guilty. Even if she enjoyed her stay with her parents she was ready to return to her own home. A few days after the wedding, Haru left her parent's home with Harish. Durgesh Panda walked with them for a mile or two. While walking with them Durgesh Panda asked Harish if he was planning to add more areas to his small house. "Why do we need a bigger place? - asked Harish curiously.

"A bigger house accommodates a bigger family" – replied the father- in- law.

Harish did not proceed any further in the discussion. He realized that Durgesh Panda wanted grandchildren. And this was a hint.

A week later, Durgesh Panda came to their house. With him he had brought a carpenter from his village who knew how to put up an addition to an existing house. Harish, his father in law and the carpenter discussed the materials needed and the cost involved. They discussed the quantity of time that was needed to complete the project. "It has to be done before the monsoon" said the carpenter.

It had been Durgesh Panda's plan all along to help Haru and her husband to build a bigger house. Before letting him marry his daughter he was fully aware of Harish's financial condition. He knew that if needed he could help the young couple. However, he waited for his younger daughter to leave home. After her wedding he was free to help his children financially. He felt that now was the time to help Haru and Harish.

Soon after their discussion, the work proceeded as planned. Durgesh Panda helped his son in law buy bamboo and timber. A couple of handymen from the village helped the carpenter. The men worked in the blazing sun. Their bony, dark bodies perspired in the heat. Sweat ran from their bodies like waterfalls. The carpenter and the workmen hammered nails, tied knots between the layers of twigs and constructed a sloping roof. They plastered the twigs with wet mud to make a smooth wall. They covered the joists on the roof with hay. In a month, their work was complete. The workmen were meticulous and paid attention to all kind of details. Their finished work made the original house look bigger. Jhumpi, Harish and Haru were pleased to see the new look of their house. Jhumpi was thankful to Durgesh Panda for helping her son. But she still wanted to retain her upper hand. As a joke she once told Durgesh "You have been aware for so long that we live in that small house. With all that money in your pocket, you should have helped us a long time ago."

Durgesh Panda laughed. "If you had a bigger house then your son- in- law would have demanded a bigger dowry" –he said.

"I was just kidding. Very few fathers have been generous to their daughters as you have been. May God bless you" said Jhumpi with genuine gratitude. This additional space had a door to the outside and could be closed from inside also. If someone came from the street to talk to Harish, which was quite often, now he could sit in the room instead of the porch. The walls were smooth. The new addition had a thatched roof. Everything looked fresh. The smell of dried mud and fresh hay gave a feeling of newness. It was exciting for Haru. She thought she could use this extra space for her classroom. The newly added space looked so lovely that Haru wished she could white wash all its walls. But doing so was expensive. She knew she could not afford the paint. Besides, it would be too noticeable in the village. Looking at a whitewashed wall, her neighbors would think that they had become rich.

Like every daughter in the world, Haru idealized her father. The way she saw him, he had worked hard for his money. She knew very well that her father was a practical man. He helped to build this new addition only because he genuinely felt they needed to have a bigger place. For him it was a natural thing to do. She did not feel any generosity on his part as her mother in law felt. As her father's daughter Haru also had developed a sense of entitlement toward his giving. Therefore, she took the whole thing in stride without any overt expression of gratitude.

On his part Durgesh Panda was happy to help his daughter and son in law. He thanked God for keeping him in a position to do so. Durgesh Panda loved his children and wanted to see them live in comfort and wealth. Like every father in the world, he felt very happy when they glowed in happiness. This was only one of the ways he wanted his daughter to be happy.

Haru settled on making colorful murals on her new walls. Pictures of a lion attacking a wild boar; Lord Ganesh with the face of an elephant and a huge belly -   sitting on the back of a mouse; Goddess Saraswati riding a peacock; and marijuana smoking Lord Shiva with a necklace of snakes adorned the walls. She used bricks, charcoal, rice flour and turmeric to make different colors like red, black, white and yellow. She combined two or three different colors to create a new one.

While the additional room was being built, occasionally Haru's class room had to be disrupted. Too much was going on. And for her, there was too much additional work to do. Her students understood the situation. And some of them chose to drop out. After the construction was finished, one by one they started trickling back. Some of them were very good – even better than Haru – in making murals on the wall. They knew how to use a brush made of rags and coconut fiber. With their help and advice Haru was able to design, paint and finish the murals. They were all delighted with the finished product.

Haru's students talked about making their own murals at home. They got ideas from each other. Some of them were even willing to go and help others who did not have much experience in making a mural. In this way a lot of houses in the village got painted walls. The pictures consisted of all kind of themes – a king leading his soldiers to fight; a dancing girl performing in front of her patrons; the sun rising through the coconut groves and mango trees; cows grazing in the pasture and many more.

It did not matter to them if the colors of the trees were black or the heads of the cows were yellow. What inspired each of the women was the desire to paint and see their own handmade products come alive on the wall. Those women knew they were not famous artists; they had no desire to be chosen as the best in that trade. What they wanted was to express themselves as carefully as they could. And they did. Their relatives, their husbands, in laws, friends and those who visited their homes appreciated their handiwork.

In the confines of a limited surrounding, getting praise from others made them proud. They had to spend many hours preparing colors for their murals and making a draft for their painting. Then they had to color the draft carefully. This took many hours. All that labor was worth every minute of it when the women received praise from their relatives and friends. Their ability to read books had built a kind of confidence they had never realized before. Now the success of their murals brought them respect. In the evening, the men folk in some of the houses were trying to read and write whereas the women folk, after finishing their cooking etc. were busy reciting their alphabets and numbers. For the first time, the village seemed to be not only peaceful but also busy. Since every one's hands were full of doing something there was no time for any one to get involved in quarrels and bickering.

The monsoon was a difficult time for everyone in the village because it brought torrential rain. The dirt roads became muddy. Walking bare feet, as they all did, was difficult. During this period every farmer had to do extra work in the field. It involved weeding out grass from the rice; applying manure to the rice field and vegetable garden; digging ditches to store rain water and making boundaries to retain necessary water in the field. If it rained continuously for several days then the cattle could not be let out and remained tied which made them antsy. Thunder scared them. At times, they acted as if they were ready to bolt. Dampness brought all kinds of bugs to their sheds. Flies were the worst. No matter how much the cattle tried to beat them with their tails, the flies never left. If an animal had a sore spot anywhere on its body then the monsoon season made the sore worse. The constant invasion of the flies was to blame. Life for the poor, who depended on daily wages, became unusually difficult. In the heavy rain outside, they could not work very much. Besides, rain and dampness always brought diseases. Runny nose, hay fever, headaches, stomach aches – all kinds of sickness became common at this time. Many of the people did not have more than two pieces of clothes to wear. So when it became damp or wet they had no other choice but continue wearing the same clothing day and night. In the absence of the sun their bodies dried their clothes in body heat.

The houses were made of mud. Sometimes the roofs leaked. The rainwater from above fell on the ground, making the dirt floor inside the house damp and miserable. Villagers suffered. But they did not know that they were suffering from any thing. For them life was as normal as it could possibly be. A desire to revolt against present hardships was simply not there with them. When the villagers found life difficult they worshipped different gods and goddesses to help them. Their unshakable faith in all kinds of deities was their strength as well as their weakness. Their faith encouraged them to move away from the tragic realities of life they faced daily. Through an abyss of escapism they attributed everything to their fate or the deeds of their previous lives.

During the monsoon period the village observed the birthdays of Lord Krishna and Lord Ganesh. It celebrated the bravery of Goddess Durga. Villagers made statues of the deities with clay and straw. They worshipped the statues whose consecration they celebrated in the village. After the occasion the statues were ceremoniously thrown into the water where they melted away to reappear the next year.

For Harish and Haru life continued in its normal way. They rose in the morning, worshipped the sun and were happy to be with each other. Harish took care of the household problems from outside whereas Haru stayed glued to the work inside the house. He went to the market and she cooked. He got the grass for the cow. She made sure the animals had enough to drink. He taught in the day and in the evening, she helped the women learn in her house. Over a period of time Haru seemed to be more and more engaged in the workings of the household. This suited Jhumpi very well. She felt relaxed. Because of Haru's competence in handling things mundane and not so mundane, she felt she could now spend more time in her Puja. Since her husband's untimely death she did not have much time to devote to worshipping or thinking about God and his creation. To her, God was someone who lived somewhere above the sky and punished people for their wrongdoing. All of her life she had been trying to do the right things not out of any fear of Him but because that is the way everything seemed to be. Now, she had more time on her hands to think about Him. She did not want to get bogged down with philosophical things. She just lived her life as best she could.

Both Harish and Haru dissuaded her to work outside on a hot day. Jhumpi did not go out to the field when the mid-day sun was too hot. When it rained, they asked her not to get too wet. They pointed out that she was getting frail and weak. Her body couldn't take all that hard work. Therefore she needed to slow down.

Their suggestions sometimes made Jhumpi angry. "I may be getting older but I am not an invalid" she thought. Therefore, she felt that her son and daughter in law should not treat her as if she were an invalid. She was not used to sitting idle. Since she was a little girl she had been working hard. After her husband died she had to be a father and a mother to her children. Now that her son is a grown man he wants to treat her like a child. "What a strange happening" she thought to herself.

While Jhumpi and her family, like their neighbors in the village, were busy attending to their affairs of life, something was taking place outside. One day, news came to the village that the

Sadhu had been arrested. A lot of people in the village speculated a lot of things as to why he was taken into police custody. But the consensus was that he was arrested because the government did not like what he said. The Sadhu had been talking about the Independence for India. So they arrested him along with a lot of other people.

For many in the village this was something incomprehensible. In their day to day life no change had ever occurred. No tradition had ever been broken. What it meant by the country's Independence, they seemed to have no clue. As far as they could see they were an independent bunch of people. Nobody told them what to do or what not to do. They got up in the morning and worked all day. Whatever came their way from the nature's bounty they accepted with pride? Yet, there was something about the recent incident that they just could not understand. The village felt the absence of the Sadhu. He was going places all the time. His being sent to jail seemed to be another of his extended journeys. Villagers continued their work as they always had. And in a few weeks, the intensity of discussion about the Sadhu's journey to jail subsided among them. Harvesting of the rice paddy from the farmland, plowing the sun baked field with a pair of bullocks yoked to a hoe, cutting the grass, grazing the cattle, celebrating religious days with puja and festivities. - were some of the familiar activities one could see in the village. Life had been going on there like this as long as one could remember. Therefore, no one expected anything to be different anytime soon.

The following year, the monsoon came early. Farmers plowed the fields and put seeds in the ground. All of them grew rice paddy. Because of the good rain the plants grew well. The farmers expected a bumper crop. At the end of the monsoon season, the crop was ready to be harvested. All the farmers in the village were anxiously waiting for their good fortune to appear in the shape of sacks and sacks of grain. But before they could harvest, it rained like cats and dogs for days. The farmers panicked. There was knee deep water in the field. The rain and the wind swept the rice plants every which way. The plants, heavy with grain drooped to the ground and fell into the standing water and rotted. The farmers knew that a continuous, heavy rain meant a severe flood. Flood meant devastation. In their minds they became sure that it was going to be a very bad year. But they did not know how bad it was going to be and they dreaded the unknown.

It had rained so much that the village pond was full to the rim. All the shallow places were waterlogged. The river seemed to swell with the run off from both sides of its banks. For several days no one could get out of the house. The cattle and the goats and the sheep were stuck in their dens. Not a single bird or a crow could fly out of its nest. All the time it was raining and raining hard. Then there was occasional thunder and lightening. It became obvious that a rainfall of this magnitude was going to cause problems. Everyone waited anxiously to see what was coming next.

They did not have to wait too long.

After the rain stopped, villagers came out of their houses. In the morning, farmers wanted to see what kind of damage had occurred to their fields and crops. Others brought out their animals to give them a break. On the whole, everyone wanted to pick up the threads of life where they had left off. Everyone knew that a good amount of rainfall was good to grow rice paddy. But this time it was devastating. The farmlands already had ankle deep water. The river was rising. More water started coming from the mountains. The situation became increasingly scary. The villagers prayed and waited to see what unfolds.

Two days later, the flood arrived and the river seemed to swell in the morning. By late afternoon that day the river had expanded itself all the way into the village. The water level kept rising. The water very quickly touched the boundary of Harish's house. The front yard where Jhumpi kept her cows tied to a post had ankle deep water. It was not healthy for the cows to remain tied in water. Harish took both the cow and calf to the yard of the temple. The ground there was a bit higher. Other villagers also had brought their animals there. For Harish it was difficult to reach the temple. The village road was covered in knee deep water. At places the current was strong. It was difficult for him to keep his balance while at the same time maneuvering the cow and the calf through the water. The animals seemed to be scared. They were mooing desperately. Finally, he managed to get to the temple yard. He was wet and worried. There, he let loose his animals. Like everybody else he pulled down a couple of knots of hay from the roof of the temple and gave them to his cattle. His mother and Haru were left home. In the face of the rising floodwater they visibly worried when he took the cow and the calf to the lawn of the temple. He did not want to keep them worried and went home to join them.

Harish was worried about their safety. "Suppose I could not get back home because of the strong current and rising water, what would happen to them?" he kept thinking. It was too painful for him to think like that. He did not want to think any further. By now everything was submerged in water. The flood had engulfed everything that was less than four feet high. Between the village road and his house lay a distance of about two hundred feet. By habit he walked straight from the road to his house. Unknown to him, the swirling water had made a big hole in the middle of the walkway. He fell into the ditch and swam his way out of it, waddling through the rising water that was swirling around him and was forcing him to swim at times, Harish finally returned home to the great relief of his wife and mother. He was exhausted and worried. At several places the river had jumped over its embankment. From a distance he could hear the gushing and roaring of the water. Harish had never seen something like this. As far as the eye could see, there was water.

The level of the flood was rising very fast. A place where children used to play or cows used to graze were submerged under god- knows- how -much water. Right outside his front yard, the floodwater was swirling and making a vortex in the strong current. He had no means of contacting any neighbors as he did not have a boat. Even if he yelled for help no one would be able to hear him. He was worried that his home would be swept away in the flood along with him, his mother and Haru.

In her life time Jhumpi had seen several floods like this. But this one seemed to be much worse than any one of them. She directed Haru to take everything off the floor and stack them on the top of the wooden chest. She feared that water was going to come inside. Once that happened things could be really out of hand. She prayed for her family's safety.

Haru had never seen a high flood like this. She had heard about trees floating in the river. But her own house would ever be swept away in the flood water was beyond her imagination. Now, for the first time, she saw the possibility of that happening. The swirling and hissing current and rising water level worried her. For strength she went up to her husband. His face looked ashen in worries and anxiety. He was still sitting on the porch with his wet clothes on. The water was about a foot away from the porch. Very silently she prayed "God, help us."

Harish realized that the floodwater would eat up the earthen porch in no time. Then the stream would run through the house. And they would perish under the floating house. He saw Haru standing by the door. "Haru, we have to climb to the roof. The situation is getting really bad."

With a ladder Harish and Haru helped Jhumpi climb up to the roof of their house. Her climbing the ladder with unsteady feet made Jhumpi feel as if she was climbing Mount Everest. Finally, she was able to reach the top of the thatched roof. Then Harish helped Haru to climb up. He was the last to go on the roof. They had taken some food with them – rice flakes and brown sugar. None of them had an appetite to eat anything. From the rooftop they could see the roaring water spread in all directions. Some of the trees with hanging branches seemed to be swimming in the water. Sounds of collapsing homes and falling trees could be heard from a distance. Their house in a sea of yellowish floodwater seemed like a speck. All three of them felt helpless and utterly worried for their safety. The late afternoon became early evening. There seemed to be no sign of the water receding. Instead the dirty water kept rising. They could see that the home that used to be their living space was now submerged in deep water. None of them had any doubt that it was just a matter of time before the entire house would collapse.

With a worried face but to divert her attention from an impending disaster Jhumpi told Harish "You should put something in your belly. All day you have not eaten anything." She had in her voice the authority that only a mother can have. Harish ignored his mother's command. He was too worried to obey her now. Besides, he had no appetite. With Jhumpi's insistence Haru brought out some rice flakes from a burlap bag. To honor the prodding of both women Harish finally ate a few rice flakes. Then Haru offered some of the flakes to her mother in law. Unwillingly, Jhumpi took some in her hand, ate a few pieces and threw the rest into the swirling water. She asked Haru to take a bite from whatever food was there. She did.

After burning itself hot and hotter all day, the sun finally began to set behind the tall coconut and palm trees. Its red and lavender rays reflected on the foamy, muddy and swirling water engulfing everything down below. From the top of the roof, Harish noticed that the water was touching the sky. All of a sudden he felt a jolt. The front wall of the house collapsed. Then the back wall came down. Instantly, the roof they were sitting on collapsed on to the water below. The three of them let out a desperate cry. He instinctively held his mother's bony left hand onto his right. Momentarily, her safety was his prime concern. Haru held on to him. With the force of the water, it felt like the roof was going to float away. But it did not. Collapsed bamboo pieces from the roof and debris from the mud walls acted like an anchor. In spite of the fall, none of them seemed to have any injury. The straws of the roof acted as a cushion.

"Mother, are you okay?" asked Harish.

Jhumpi did not reply because she could not. The fact that her son and daughter in law safely survived the collapse of their house made her thankful. She was relieved to see them unharmed. At the same time she was sad to see her house destroyed in the flood- water.

When Harish's eyes met with Haru's he saw a sense of melancholy in her eyes. She tightly held on to his hand. Both of them seemed to be on the verge of crying.

The following morning, around daybreak, the water seemed to recede. The three of them had rested all night on the collapsed thatched roof. Hardly could sleep come to their eyes. For a while Haru had rested her head on her husband's lap. She was dozing off and on. All of a sudden she felt a pain in her stomach and let out projectile vomiting. Harish became nervous. If she were sick, he did not know what to do or how to help her at this moment. In a very worried voice he asked her "How are you feeling?"

Haru did not want to make her husband worried any further. Besides, they were all victims of the flood. She replied "I am fine"

Jhumpi was wide awake. She had not noticed any sickness in Haru's face. Her throwing up at this moment seemed unusual to her. Haru's confession that she was fine told her something totally new. In spite of all the destruction presently around her, for the first time in a long period in her life Jhumpi felt happy. Something from her own experience told her that Haru's projectile vomiting was a sign that she was pregnant. Jhumpi could barely resist her glee now. She burst out laughing like a crazy woman. In total bewilderment, Harish looked at his mother. She was still laughing. "What is it mother?" he asked. "I am going to be a grandmother," came her prompt reply.

6

After the flood receded, villagers were able to come out of their marooned habitats. They had been living in isolation, although in some places several families had huddled together for safety. In face of the rising and swirling water all of them seemed to have hung on to their dear lives and each other. For all of them, the first order of business was to assess the devastation. There was not a single house standing anywhere in the village. Their roofs lay on the ground in mud. The wells from where villagers drew drinking water now overflowed with dirty water. Grains and foodstuff were usually hard to find in good times. Now they were all washed away or rotted in the dirty water. Precious little food could be found readily. Those who were relatively well off managed to possess some staple. But for the poor people it was difficult to find any.

The entire area remained cut off from the outside world

because of the water. Those who did not have enough food before the flood had much less now. The poor with children suffered the most. It was a heartbreaking experience for the mothers in those families. The children had been scared in the face of the rising water. Now, the panic in their faces reflected the panic of their parents. The children had no idea how serious the flood was or what its impact would be. They got strength from the presence of their parents. But the parents were worried to death for them. The children were hungry. They cried and went to sleep in their parent's laps without food. It was somewhat bearable for an adult to go without. But it was heart wrenching to see a child cry for food where there is none and finally goes to asleep tired.

Both the well to do and the poor of the village shared a common fate now. They were both in the same situation. Desperate and broken hearted they tried to pick up the pieces. Whoever had anything edible shared it with others. They all tried to survive together in a very cruel situation.

Every family needed to raise their fallen roofs and collapsed walls. Labor was hard to get in a situation like this because every one needed help. Those who were skilled to do this kind of work were generally poor. They themselves needed to raise their roofs and fix their collapsed walls. But they had to feed their children first. So they worked for others all day and did their own work in their spare time. Those who could afford hired them as help.

With assistance from others Harish was able to raise the roof of his house. With palm leaves he made temporary walls and lay boards on the damp floor. Like everybody else in the entire area he tried to make do with whatever was available and it was not much. Compared to many other families he was rather lucky. His mother had squirreled away enough rice that would feed three of them for two more months. She had kept the rice in large burlap bags. Floodwater made the bags wet. But the rice could be dried. That is what both Haru and Jhumpi did. After the flood they dried their rice in the open sun. There were too many families who had nothing to eat. So, the two of them were very careful not to be too obvious about their possession. There were families who were having a very rough time in feeding their children. Occasionally one of them would come to borrow rice from them. The needy families knew that Haru would be kinder than her mother in law. So they would try to approach her first. But she would refer them to Jhumpi.

First of all, Haru did not want to project herself as the decision-maker of the household. Secondly, she could not go out to collect the IOUs but her mother in law could. Over the years Jhumpi had known every family of the village. She knew who needed help and who could be counted on returning a favor. She had seen their honesty, thankfulness as well as their thankless behavior. In a time like this she could not afford to judge them. They all had children. For the children's sake, even if her heart did not want to listen to their pathetic stories, Jhumpi loaned them rice. "I did not want to see her face. But she has children. What can I do?" she would lament to Haru after the borrower had left.

Not only the village but the entire area lost its main crop rice paddy. Growing rice needed a lot of rain and the monsoon was the right time for its cultivation. After the monsoon, growing rice, the staple, was risky. The villagers were not risk takers. In spite of all the damage the flood had done, it brought with it sediments from faraway places and deposited it on the farmland and made the land fertile for winter crops.

The flood had broken the back of every family in the village. The crop was gone. With this was gone the entire season's labor and hope. Their savings of staples and their houses also had been destroyed. It was the loss of the house that wrought devastation. There were memories of wedding, child- birth, puja and festivity. In a sudden stroke of a bad hand of nature all of that was washed away. This hurt the people of the village the most. Slowly, as the loss sunk in, an utter hopelessness blanketed every life and every household. Before the flood, villagers were doing many things to enjoy life and keep themselves busy. There was exuberance everywhere. But now the face of the village looked different. It was full of collapsed homes and ruined dreams. Helplessness blanketed the air. In a time like this everyone wished the presence of the Sadhu among them. "But he is in jail" they told one another.

The Sadhu was like a lighthouse, a guiding force. He did not have money to give away or a lot of materials to distribute. But he could spread the message of their difficulties in far away places. He could have asked others for help on their behalf. He generated hope and hope was something that all of them needed at a time like this.

After the flood, the first casualty was Harish's evening school. All his pupils were busy taking care of problems at hand. No one had any desire to sit and read in the evening. In view of the colossal problems his pupils faced to feed their families and build their houses, efforts to read and write seemed to be unimportant. Besides, all the crops they could gather were destroyed. However, the children's day school still continued. It had gotten support from the village, but as the crop was washed away, a lot of families could not afford to pay the fees for their children anymore. They stopped sending them to school. As the enrollment at the school decreased so did Harish's financial fortune. Haru's women's group also stopped coming.

Jhumpi's cow did not do very well after the flood. Because of water everywhere it was difficult to find green grass. When people don't have enough to eat they can't pay too much attention to the welfare of their cattle. All of the rice juice, left over vegetables, lentil husks and bean skins that the cow used to eat were not available any more. There was no grass for the cow. The only food it could get was leaves cut from different trees and the stored up straw. By the time the flood arrived the cow was a few months pregnant. Anxiety and trauma from the sea of water accompanied by lack of proper feeding made her abort. Jhumpi had plans about the cow. She had hoped to sell the milk and milk products. But the miscarriage of the cow ruined her hopes. The flood destroyed her plan.

The animal was like a member of her family. As a mother,

she felt the grieving cow's loss and sympathized with her. To Jhumpi, the animal's vacant look and helpless mooing told everything. In sympathy Jhumpi often massaged the cow's neck and whispered to her repeatedly "It will be alright. It will be alright." There seemed to be instant communication between the two of them. When Jhumpi ran her hand over the cow's neck or touched its body the cow became still and quiet. It felt her affection. Jhumpi gave the cow whatever straw or leaves she could gather.

Soon after the floodwater receded, the rumor swirled around that so and so village had cases of cholera. Everyone in the village knew that this was a dangerous and communicable disease and it could kill. The fear of death increased villagers' worries. They arranged collective prayers. Because of their present situation they could not do their pujas on a grand scale to please the gods. But in their hearts and minds they prayed desperately. Someone coming from another village told them that in his village every family had been boiling their water to avoid the disease and it had worked. Encouraged by this account the villagers started doing the same and waited for the resulst. They were thankful that the disease did not arrive in their village.

In a few months the river began to dry and where the people used to cross by a boat, now they started crossing on foot. The farmers in the village started tilling their lands for the winter crop. Slowly, the old routine of the village life began to return. But this time it was different. There was not enough food to go around. There was not enough work for those who did not own any land and depended on working for others. Everyone was worried about rebuilding his house. There was an underlying sadness in every one's life.

This was a very different time for Haru. She was pregnant. Her mother in law had guessed it right about her vomiting. Haru did not know then why she was feeling that way. She thought maybe it was the anxiety from the flood. But the older woman seemed to know exactly what it was.

Jhumpi insisted that her daughter in law in this present

condition be more careful while walking in the mud; she offer a certain kind of puja for specific gods and goddesses that she did not do before and she take a nap in the middle of the day. As usual the older woman was full of dos and don'ts. This time, ever since she discovered Haru's pregnancy her list of do's and don'ts seemed to get longer. The mother in law made sure that Haru ate well. She would ask Harish to bring specific fruits and vegetables for Haru. She would ask him to do some chores in and around the house so that Haru did not have to strain herself. Jhumpi always kept a watchful eye on her daughter- in- law.

As the months went by Haru became rounder. She ran her hand over her protruding stomach to feel the baby inside. She was careful, very careful in lifting heavy things like a big water pot. She stopped drawing water from the well altogether. Harish's additional workload around the house bothered Haru. She knew her husband worked hard outside. So she was ashamed to make him work hard inside the house. She would protest

"No, mother I can do that".

"Don't worry, you will have plenty of time to do such chores after the baby comes" her mother in law would reply.

Harish was happy to help around the house. He did not mind.

As her pregnancy progressed, Haru's movements became increasingly slower. She couldn't do much of the cooking. With a lot of prayer and anxiety she kept waiting for her baby to be born. She ate a lot and slept a lot and tried to obey all the dos and don'ts laid down by her mother- in- law. She often felt as if the baby was talking to her. Haru felt all the fear and anxiety of an expectant mother. But her mother in law took all of this in stride. As Jhumpi saw it, child bearing was a fact of life for a young woman. Every woman of a certain age went through this experience. She had gone through this in her time. So now it was Haru's turn. From her experience she also knew that a young woman, being pregnant for the first time, is scared and worried and needs all the support and good wishes she could get. Still the experience is a very lonely one and cannot be transferred from one person to another.

Jhumpi felt it was her responsibility as a mother in law to give Haru all the support she needed at this time. Therefore, she went out of her way to make things easier for her. She drew water from the well, cleaned husks from the rice paddy, made cow dung patties so that Haru did not have to strain herself too much. There was one thing that Haru enjoyed very much and that was cooking. Jhumpi also knew Haru's cooking tastes better than the cooking of her own. Therefore, she let her cook most of the time.

Haru's parents often sent her tasty foods and inquired about her health. A visit from her father or any of the brothers was reassuring for her. Slowly but certainly, Haru's stomach continued to look bigger. All the women in the village and their husbands and in laws came to know about it. The women exchanged facts and told stories of their experiences. Haru listened to them, laughed with them and prayed that she did not have to go through the awful misery some of the women had. She prayed for herself and her baby – she prayed more for her baby than for herself. Inside her the baby continued to grow. As the day of delivery drew closer, the level of her anxiety increased. In spite of everybody around her she felt increasingly lonely and overwhelmed.

For Harish this was a completely new experience. He enjoyed the idea that very soon he was going to be a father. Haru's misery of being pregnant bothered him. Yet, there was very little he could do. To give her support and strength he often held her hand and kissed her. He let her rest her head on his shoulder and held her tightly. He did all this only when his mother was not around. The modesty of the village life prevented public display of such affection between a wife and her husband. Looking at her enlarged belly he would jokingly ask "Haru, how did this happen?" And then both of them would burst out laughing. He would run his hand over Haru's belly. He would try to listen to the baby's movement. And then comment "I think the baby is singing."

Then they would laugh again. Haru would hold his hand tightly. "Don't worry, Haru. Everything would be alright" Harish would assure his wife. She would nod with him. He would bring

Haru's favorite fruits and vegetables like jackfruit, pineapple, cantaloupe, eggplant, white pumpkin and sour fruit. He would bring her different kinds of green leaves and ripe berries. Haru would cook the vegetables and greens. She would wash and serve the fruits and berries. She would not try some of them because of fear that they might upset the baby. From the fresh fruits she would try some. But before taking some for herself she would always make sure that her mother in law got some. "Look, you are the pregnant one. Why, are you giving me all this?" Jhupmi would question her in mock annoyance to which Haru would just laugh.

Haru's anxiety and Jhumpi's excitement seemed to run on a parallel track. The reality that she was going to have a grandchild made Jhumpi very happy. One day she would have a chance to hold her grandchild in her arms; she would walk with the child to the temple; she would tell stories; above all else she would pamper the baby with all her love. The above possibilities tickled her mind to no end. But there were practical things that she had to arrange for the unborn.

The village had no doctor so for delivering babies, expectant mothers and in- laws depended on a woman who practiced child-delivery in her spare time. Her name was Rambha. She lived at the end of the village in a mud hut. At her real work, Rambha wove baskets from bamboo. Delivering babies meant touching blood and feces which in the prevalent ways of thinking was dirty work. Therefore, no woman from the upper castes would do such a job. Rambha had neither training nor education about handling deliveries. Having had several children of her own she knew that at the time of birth the mother has to push the baby from inside. Once the head is out the rest of the body of the baby needs to be pulled out. Her main role in the birthing situation was to yell "push", as hard and as convincingly as she could. She carried her special knife to cut the umbilical curd. At home, Rambha kept the knife under wraps. After using it she washed the knife in water and repeatedly smeared ash on it. The knife looked reasonably sharp. No one in the village ever kept count as to how many babies were born or how many of them died at birth. Everything happened under the watchful eyes of gods and goddesses. All births and deaths depended on their mercy or anger. Therefore, no one ever questioned Rambha's helping hand. Regardless of her skill level, every one was thankful for her presence at a critical time like this.

Jhumpi alerted Rambha about the future birth of her grand child. Rambha gave the prospective grandmother a list of things to keep handy for the day. The materials included plenty of turmeric paste, dried ginger roots, sandal wood, castor oil, cowdung cakes to make a fire, a hurricane lantern and three oil lamps. Way before Haru's due date Jhumpi collected all the materials. Turmeric paste would dry up. Therefore, she kept a lot of turmeric roots at hand. Periodically Jhumpi checked and rechecked that all the things were on hand. She was pleased to find that not a thing from Rambha's list was amiss.

While Haru was going through pains and anticipations of pregnancy and Jhumpi was burning with hope for the future, Harish's financial situation was not going very well. After the flood every family in the area was going through a rough time. No one seemed to have any money to spend. Finding food and other essentials was keeping everyone busy. In a situation like this, sending children for schooling was the lowest of priorities. Harish was not getting as many students in his day class. And the evening school had stopped right after the flood. His income was dwindling. He was not a farmer. He did not have a lot of land and whatever land he inherited was a small patch of earth that lay ruined in the flood and could not support his family anyway. It was difficult for him to imagine how he was going to improve his income. After the flood the village seemed to have changed forever. Every man under certain age who had a family to feed was concerned about making ends meet. Food was the most urgently needed thing. Yet there was not enough to go around. Very few could afford to buy because no one seemed to have any money.

The situation was becoming hopeless and out of this desperation each of them had to carve out a slice of the future

Several young men from the village were planning to leave for Calcutta. It was far away from the village. But Calcutta was full of opportunities. Harish thought he could make money by doing puja in houses of rich people there. The rich in the big city had money. Unlike the village folks they rolled in wealth. And he was sure that he would not have any problem getting largess from them. If nothing came his way then he could work in the jute mills of Calcutta. His mother would not approve of his work as a laborer. But she wouldn't know what it meant to work in a jute mill anyway. As long as he could send some money for her on a regular basis she would forgive him. Besides, Calcutta was far away. No one in the village would know what he did or did not do there.

As he thought about improving his economic situation he became more and more certain that going to Calcutta to try his luck was not only the best solution, it was the only solution. He had never lived outside the village. Now the prospect of living in Calcutta brought certain uncertainty into his mind. He had to leave Haru and his mother in the village. The baby would come. He would not be able to spend all his time with his child. He wished there was another way. But there was none.

Harish could not discuss his ideas with his mother. He knew that she would be very unhappy. She would probably weep by learning that he was planning to leave for Calcutta. He did not want to make Haru worried either. She was so vulnerable now! Harish had no heart to tell her that he was planning to leave the village. Several men from nearby villages had gone there to make a living. They had done reasonably well. The example of their exodus from the village had not gone unnoticed by others. Each of them had parents and children and a wife at home. However, Harish could not leave just before the birth of his first child. So he waited.

On learning that her sister was going to have her first baby, Paru sent her a letter inquiring how she was doing. "I am ready and desperate to bring this brat out. 'Mother' says it is a girl. The brat has already started kicking. Now, I look like a big jackfruit or an oversize watermelon – big and bloated." wrote back Haru. She showed it to Harish.

"You don't look like a jackfruit or a watermelon. You look lovely" he commented.

Finally, the baby was ready to arrive on time. Before Haru's water broke, Rambha was summoned to the house. Haru kept screaming and sweating in pain. Rambha, with all of her experience, kept on cajoling her to push and breathe hard. She lent her hands for the young mother to hold tightly. Rambha was gentle and encouraging and full of assurance. With her help Haru delivered a little girl. Throughout her ordeal Jhumpi was at her daughter in law's side. She kept on assuring her "Everything will be alright. Don't worry. You will be fine." When the little baby on her arrival let out a big scream, Jhumpi felt like her head touched the heavens. "God bless the baby" she cried out loudly. After giving birth, Haru, like a rain soaked flower, exhausted but still pretty fell asleep. Rambha and Jhumpi washed the baby, cut her umbilical cord and gave her warmth by wrapping in clean rags. By the time Haru woke up she found a tiny human being lying next to her. After crying her lungs out the baby had fallen asleep. The tiny little thing was all flesh. The first thing Haru noticed of the baby was her sharp nose and a thick bunch of hair. Haru bent down to kiss her. At that moment the baby awakened and once again burst out a big cry. "It is going to wake up the whole neighborhood" – Jokingly commented the proud grandmother and suggested to Haru "She is hungry." Haru breast fed her baby for the first time.

Everyone in the family loved the newborn. In the evenings Jhumpi rubbed the baby's body with turmeric paste and washed her in warm water. She made sure that the young mother took proper care of herself. Since the mother was nursing the baby, the baby's health depended on her. Therefore, she made sure that Haru ate properly and kept her environment spotlessly clean. In order to ward off the mosquitoes that swarmed in the dark Jhumpi made a smolderingly low fire with cow dung patties inside the house and burned incense.

It took a few days for Haru to overcome her weakness. She knew it would be longer for her to get back to normal. During Haru's recovery period, which seemed to her like ages, her mother in law did all the cooking and cleaning that needed to be done in the house. She had not done those things for ages. And she stumbled while doing them. All the time she was happy for the arrival of the baby.

The new addition to the family meant additional needs. In spite of becoming a proud father Harish was nervous and worried. Haru had gained her strength back and the baby was becoming bigger by the day. His mother seemed to be spending all her waking hours caring for the baby. Convinced that Haru could handle the blow now, Harish finally told her of his intention. Haru had articulated their financial situation very well. She was not surprised by what he said. She just looked at him. She wanted him to be home with her all the time. She dreaded her bed without him. But she also knew her husband had responsibilities. "I am with you in whatever you decide" said she in a very low voice.

After getting the green light from Haru it was not difficult for Harish to convince his mother of his journey to Calcutta. At first she was bewildered about his plan. But she too was realistic. The mother realized that her son now had four mouths to feed. He must repair the ruined house. Doing all this required money. After the devastating flood in the area he was unable to find money in the village. So he had to do something different.

"Hope, you would have enough money to attend my funeral when I die" said the mother.

"Don't worry, Mother. I will attend your funeral no matter what" said her son.

Sometimes later, Harish left for Calcutta leaving behind his three - month- old daughter with his wife and mother.

7

Arriving at the train station in Howrah, Harish found himself in a crowd of people wearing all kinds of clothes. They spoke languages he did not understand. In the train he had met people who seemed to be quite unlike the people of his village. But for the most part the compartment in his train was full of people who looked like him, wore the same kind of clothes as he did and spoke the language he spoke. But Howrah, the main train station of Calcutta, was different, quite different, unlike anything he had ever seen.

Harish was not familiar with the big city. He had never visited any town or city before. He came to Calcutta because he could not make a living in his village. His mind was full of anticipation. His heart was beating fast. He had made arrangements with a friend to meet him at the station. All the time, while travelling, he was worried whether or not the friend from his village would remember. He was praying with all his heart for the friend to meet him at the train station. After buying the ticket to Calcutta he had no money left with him. Returning home was out of the question. No matter what, he had to stay in Calcutta to make a living. If it meant he had to live on the street he was ready to do that.

Everybody in the Howrah station was disembarking from the train. The car was getting empty. One of his co-passengers assured him that they had reached the final destination, Calcutta. Harish got up and followed the passengers who seemed to be going in one direction only. There was a big iron gate where a man with a big mustache was collecting tickets. Harish handed the used ticket to him. As soon as he came out of the big iron gate he saw his friend Jamu who had been waiting for him there for a couple of hours. For Harish, it was a big relief. Both of them walked to Jamu's residence. The place was about an hour's walk. Walking was no big deal for either of them. In the village they walked all the time and everywhere. The only problem was that this time, Harish carried a load on his back. He had a few clothes and some other belongings in a burlap bag that he had tied in a knot. He placed the load on his back and walked along the side of his friend. There seemed to be too many people everywhere and around him. All of them seemed to be crossing the same street over and over. He had no idea where they were all going or coming from.

Harish kept following his friend. Finally they stopped in front of a one story building that looked like a barracks with a dozen or so rooms. Each room had one door to the front. There was no window in any of them. Ever so many people came and went out of the individual rooms. The air was filled with the smell of burning charcoal. It was mid- morning. People were getting ready to go to their businesses. A few women were cooking food. Someone was frying onions in oil. Another one was cooking rice and dhal. Someone else was frying fish. The combined odor of all of this mixed with the smell of burning charcoals created a strange smell for Harish. He had no heart to complain. Harish knew that in order to survive in Calcutta this is something he had to get used to. He had spent a whole day walking to catch the train to Calcutta. Then all night he sat up with no sleep. He had heard of stories about people being robbed and pick-pocketed while traveling. Therefore he was determined to stay awake to protect whatever he had with him.

Now, his body was exhausted and he needed a few hours' sleep to recuperate. Jamu had to go to work. After dropping him off in the room he gave Harish a key to lock the door in case he had to go out. Harish learned that there were four other souls living in that same room. Presently, they had all gone to work. Harish tried to sleep. It was a bright day and a lot of noise was coming from all sides. The place was new and totally unfamiliar to him. He felt anxious in the big city. Then the thought of Haru, the baby and his mother took over his mind. Without them he felt terribly lonely. Harish felt as if he was going to cry.

In the evening all of the residents of the rooming house, which everyone referred to as a 'mess' came "home". They all spoke the same language, Oriya. But they belonged to different castes from different areas. All of them were about the same age. Before coming to Calcutta they lived in a remote village like his. Each of them had a family back home. They were here to make money. Each of them once was a new comer. So they shared with Harish their experiences of being new in Calcutta. "Anyone willing to work hard can make a few pennies here" said one of them to which all of them agreed. That evening, Harish and his friend Jamu took a walk around their immediate area. The first thing Harish noticed that unlike his village, there were very few trees around. Then there were a lot of houses made of bricks and cement; very few had thatched roofs. What surprised him most was the number of women walking on the street who went on their businesses like men without covering their faces. Some of them wore clothes that showed their legs. Instead of wearing dhoti some of the men wore pajamas and shirts. Because of their garb the men seemed threatening to him.

With Jamu he discussed his future. Harish knew what to do. But he had no idea how to start. Jamu had been in Calcutta for a while. He sold flowers on the street. Every day he went to a particular small wholesaler to buy roses with long stems. He moved from street to street selling his roses until the entire stock was sold. His profit margin was good and some days he made some real money." Selling flowers on the street was a tough business involving a lot of hard work. So he was a kind of pro about the life in the city. In clear conscience he could not suggest such a job for Harish. He knew Harish was more cerebral and should have a job that suited his education and upbringing. He suggested to Harish that God willing he could work as an apprentice to a priest in a nearby temple.

The idea appealed to Harish. He thought even if he might not be able to impress the priest because of their language difference he could certainly talk in Sanskrit to the deities in the temple.

The following morning, with the conviction of a prizefighter, Harish went to the priest of the nearby temple. In broken Hindi he was able to relay to the priest that he was looking for a job as an apprentice. The priest was kind. He asked Harish about his background and education. He asked about Harish's family life. The priest was an older man. With sandalwood paste on his forehead he looked distinguished. For whatever reason he took a liking for Harish whose sincere way of talking and humility impressed him. He saw a sense of desperation in the young man's voice. The priest was moved and became willing to help. His temple was not rich enough to support an apprentice. But he knew a few very rich people who had private temples inside the compounds of their palatial houses. Others possessed the statue of a deity in a corner of their homes. All of them needed someone to come daily to worship the deities properly. He himself was busy looking after the puja arrangements at the temple. This was round the clock work. Making rounds to all those homes was getting a bit too much for him. The priest was willing to introduce Harish to some of those families.

Within a week of the conversation with the priest at the temple, Harish had a client base of twelve families. When he visited their homes and temples daily he was greeted with respect. The families offered him sweets and staples. They offered him generous amount of money. Slowly he became convinced that Calcutta was going to be good for him. He saw a bright future for himself in the big city.

Like everybody else in the city trying to make a living, Harish developed a schedule for himself. He woke up early in the morning, before sunrise; dipped into the water of the Hughli by walking to its banks for a mile or so and recited his mantras on his way back from the river. At the rooming house he did his personal puja that consisted of reading sacred verses from various holy books and reciting many sacred verses from memory. Then he went to different homes and worshipped the deities. The families offered him food and tea. He returned "home" in the evening.

Soon, Harish became known in the immediate community for his ability to conduct religious functions. He blessed his clients for their welfare. He fervently pleaded their wishes before the deities – wellness of an ailing child, victory in a legal dispute, promotion at a job, sale of a valuable property; and so on. He did his clients' pleading before the deities so convincingly that in a short period of time he became a sought-after individual by many. Not only did the rich families call him but many not so rich also needed his help. Since every one had a favorite God or Goddess to ask for blessings they all wanted Harish's help to please the deity. If a worshipper was successful in getting his or her wish fulfilled then he or she was convinced that it happened because of Harish's fervent pleading before the heavenly power. If it did not happen then it was due to bad luck. More pujas were needed to straighten up the situation. Before completing one month in Calcutta, Harish was able to send 30 rupees home. It was the most money he had ever seen at one time.

For the entire month he had been thinking about Haru, the

baby and his mother. He was worried about how they were managing in the village. By sending them money he felt better.

In the village his family was anxious about him. Both Jhumpi and Haru in their own way worried about his health and safety. They were not sure what kind of financial strength he would have. When the mailman brought the money order to their house they were overjoyed. Jhumpi wanted to know from the mailman if there was a letter from her son. She had forgotten that she received a letter from him a couple of days ago. The mailman handed her the money but no letter. She felt good when she held the cash in her hand. Yet, she wished her son were in the village. "Money or not, just seeing him every day would have been more fulfilling" she thought. Jhumpi took the money and handed the entire sum to her daughter in law.

"Why are you giving me all this money?" asked Haru.

"Look, I am getting old. I can't keep account of all of this. My son has sent it. This is all yours"– Replied Jhumpi. She picked up her granddaughter from her mat and took her outside the house to let her play. Ever since Harish left for Calcutta, Jhumpi had been feeling a kind of loss that only a mother can feel. Whenever she felt like crying she would pick up her granddaughter and caress her. Just looking at the baby would remind her of Harish and she would forget her agony for the time being.

On Haru's part, life was immeasurably difficult. For the first few days after her husband left for Calcutta she could not sleep. Until his letter arrived in the village announcing that he had reached there safely she was on pins and needles. She did not know how it felt traveling on a train. She did not know what the people of Calcutta were like. Whether or not he was safe she did not know. She was worried to death. His safe arrival finally put her anxiety to rest. His presence in the village and around the house had been a big strength for her. She missed that badly. Now, she had to depend on hired hands to fix this or repair that. In bed she missed her husband terribly.

Days became weeks and weeks became months. Harish stayed in Calcutta and Haru lived in the village with her daughter whom they had named Sudha, meaning nectar. The baby seemed to be growing rapidly. When Harish left, the baby could hardly turn over. Now she was able to do many tricks. Haru imagined how happy Harish would have been to see his daughter when for the first time she sat up or stood or started talking. But he was not there. Therefore, she could only imagine his laughter and his joy. Everyday, in her thoughts, Haru wrote a letter to her husband. It had all kind of things. She wanted to let him know how she missed him in her day- to- day life. She missed his touch. She missed his voice, the sounds of his steps on the porch. She wanted to tell him that the baby is in good health and had started saying "ba-ba" "ma-ma". She wanted to let him know how lonely she feels without him around. Cooking has not been fun any more. Without his presence around the house, mother and she have been managing somehow.

After receiving the money Haru had to write a letter. The post office did not have stamps, or envelopes. They were expensive. Therefore, every one in the village used post cards which were cheap. But this could hold fewer words. Any outsider could read the postcard. Therefore, she could not bring herself to write all her inner feelings on it. Haru's letter consisted of a bare minimum of personal information. She decided to save her feelings for their personal encounter. Now she just let him know about the baby's health, mother's health, how they are buying rice paddy and lentils etc. because of the low price after the harvest. She also wrote him about her parents. She mentioned Sumi and her family because she knew that he always wanted to know about his sister.

It was a common sight not only in her village but also in many other villages that men went to far away places to make a living while their wives languished at home. The men earned and sent money home regularly. Both the husband and the wife suffered the cruelty of separation. Yet, both realized the necessity of it. Haru was experiencing the same thing in her own life. In spite of all the loneliness and all the heartache that came with this self -imposed but necessary living-apart she was gathering courage within herself to face the future. It appeared to her that her husband and she were going to live in two different corners of the world regardless of how much they loved each other or how much they missed one another.

Slowly, Sudha was growing up. From an infant she had become a toddler. Slowly she was becoming a little girl trying to explore things, learning about everyone and every thing around her. Haru was writing letters to her husband about the progress of their child. She was waiting for a letter from him almost every day. Whenever the mailman, known as "post peon", came to their neighborhood she expected to get a letter from her husband. If it actually came she would be uncontrollably happy. If it did not then she would feel miserable. All kind of anxiety would fill her heart. It was not the letter that mattered much. It was the sensation of something that bore Harish's name that mattered to her the most. All the while Haru kept herself engaged in the chores of the house. But her mind was always stuck somewhere in a far away place called Calcutta.

As weeks and months went by people in the village began to recuperate from the impact of the severe flood. They grew crops and raised livestock. Jhumpi's cow had a new calf. She started milking again. Sometimes, she would go to the field to collect grass for her pet cow. If it was too hot or if she were under the weather then Haru would dissuade her to work in the field. Sometimes Haru's suggestions worked. Most often they did not. Jhumpi was sure that the cow needed green grass to give good milk. Therefore she was not going to sit home for nothing. If she could, she always tried to get grass for the cow.

Sudha and the cow became friends. Holding her in one arm Jhumpi let her touch the cow's back. To her soft little palms the cow felt wooly and hard. When she touched the cow's horn it nodded in disagreement. Slowly she learned to tease the animal by repeatedly touching its horns. On the other hand the cow got used to Sudha's touch and did not get disturbed any more. The cow kind of expected such a touch from her. From a safe place like her grandmother's arm the little girl felt a sense of entitlement to do anything to the cow including touching its horn whether the cow liked it or not. As the protector of both, Jhumpi became the arbitrator between them. When the cow was in a disagreeable mood she did not let Sudha touch her and did not bring her near the cow. Very early on Sudha learned that the cow loved to eat. So whenever she felt full and did not want to eat she gave the rest to the animal. This irritated Haru. But she enjoyed her daughter's fondness for the cow.

Letters and money regularly came from Harish. He always asked about Sudha. For Haru he always had a lot of suggestions. Slowly it occurred to Haru that while he was in Calcutta and trying to make a living there, it was she who had to look after everything back in the village. She had to fill a dual role. A lot of things that Harish would have been doing, either she had to do or get it done through someone else. Or shoe could let it go undone. Her mother-in- law could not be counted on to do it anymore. Between the cow and Sudha she was always busy. Besides, now-a-days she had taken up all kinds of puja and fasting. She had little spare time to look after anything in the house. The house keys she so carefully used to keep tied to the end of her sari were no longer with her. Long ago, she entrusted those to Haru. As the most senior member of the household her mother in law still retained the authority in the house. But actual management, looking after the details of things and getting things done fell on her. She had nothing to complain about. It was her house and her husband was away on a mission. She had to get done all that needed to be done.

After a year, Harish returned to his village for the first time. He wore clean white clothes. He wore a white, short sleeve shirt. In the intervening year he seemed to have changed a lot. People in the village, mostly his friends and former students, were curious to know about life in the city. They were interested in knowing about his lifestyle there. None of them had ever left the village. The most distance they had traveled was to a relative's house a few miles away. Calcutta was a big place and too far away. For them, it had allurement of a mythic proportion. Harish told them about tall buildings, roads without mud, and women walking on the street with men folk. He was a good narrator. His description of things and incidents were accurate. In a way Harish tried to give his listeners a clear picture of the city and its life. He was glad to be back in the village for a short while. At the same time he knew that his fate was tied to Calcutta.

While in the village he played with Sudha. He disciplined her when it was necessary and enjoyed every minute of her presence in his life. Sudha was very happy to see this new man in her life. Now she was more than one year old and growing. She was healthy and beautiful. Looking at her chubby cheeks and beautiful black eyes Harish thought she was from another world. Besides, Sudha had such a wonderful smile. When she smiled the entire world seemed to giggle. This was the part Harish enjoyed the most.

After a month of stay in the village he prepared to return to Calcutta. He knew he would miss his family. He became sad to leave the village. At the same time he was proud of his financial achievements. He could buy things for his wife and daughter. This time he had brought a bottle of scented oil, a cake of soap and several new saris for Haru. She liked all of them. Living in the village he could not afford those things. First of all those things could not be found in the village. Secondly, where would he find the money to buy them anyway? Both happiness and sadness seemed to mix in his mind and create a sense of melancholy.

The week before he had to leave, Haru seemed to be in a miserable state of mind. In fear that she was going to lose him again she became very sad and lost her appetite. She did her chores around the house and to an outsider she looked normal. But inside she seemed to be consumed by fear and apprehension. It was the impending loneliness that was killing her inside. She wished her husband did not have to leave. But there was no way for her to hold him back.

The night before Harish's departure Haru cried a lot. Holding hands and leaning on each other they talked very late into the night and finally Harish fell asleep. But Haru could not. All night she stayed awake. She tossed and turned in the bed. Haru in her very selfish way wished this particular night would never end so that she and Harish could lie there for hours and days. But that was not to be. The dawn came with a vengeance. Once again the world lit up with sunlight. The birds chirped, the cows mooed and a stray dog here and there started barking. People started going about their business. Now she had to face the world. Harish had to leave for Calcutta. She had to pack his things.

When Haru left the bed, her eyes were red due to lack of sleep and for crying.

When Harish saw her face he felt a kind of stabbing in his heart. Yet he had to be strong. So looking at his wife he said" Haru you have to be strong. If you cry like this it will not be good for me."

"I know" said Haru . She looked away so that her husband would not see the tears running from her eyes. Secretly she wiped her tears. At that moment she wanted to be strong. A realization came to her that for years to come this kind of separation was going to be a fact of life and she had to be ready for this. Once again she smiled broadly at Harish.

The last time when Harish left home he did not know what to expect in the big city. So he had taken a lot of things from home. This time he lived in Calcutta and knew what to expect. Therefore, he did not take too many unnecessary things. But his mother packed him some ghee that she had made from her butter. Haru sent some fried dough and pickles. Harish liked pickles and he knew that her homemade pickles was going to last him for months. But fried dough would quickly become stale. He knew he would share this with his roommates. Harish left his village in the middle of the morning before the sun was too hot and walked all day to the nearest train station. He was to catch the evening train to Calcutta. This time he seemed to be less anxious and less apprehensive. In the hot sun of the noon the road under his feet felt very uncomfortable like burning earth. His bag was heavier than he wanted. So when the sun became unbearable and he felt exhausted Harish rested under a tree for a few minutes. Once again, he kept walking. The sun also made him thirsty. There were wells at different points on the road. If there was a bucket attached to a rope then he drew water from the well and drank to his heart's content. He did not want to eat while he still had miles to cover. Harish feared that if he took time to eat then it would slow him down and he would miss his train.

By the time he arrived at the station he was tired and hungry. He opened the packet Haru had sent with him for the road. He opened it carefully. Haru had sent some sweets and fried dough. Harish ate the food and drank a tall glass of water and waited for the train to arrive. In a couple of hours the train came. And with his ticket in hand he boarded it for Calcutta, his destination and destiny.

8

The priest of the temple was a well-liked man. Many important people of the area came to his temple on auspicious days and made it a point to see him and get blessings from him. Harish had his goodwill. Through the priest of the temple he was able to meet a lot of good people. The contacts helped him and opened new doors. Slowly, Harish's circle of acquaintance began to expand. When he visited different families to perform Puja he also came to know their servants along with their visiting relatives

Calcutta was a big city. It had many important and not so important people. Harish was there only to make a living and to help improve his lot in the village. He began to like the life in Calcutta and became a part of its hustle and bustle and began enjoying its hue and cry. After a whole day of running around, when he returned to the rooming house in the evening, he seemed to have many stories to tell his friends. His friends too had their own stories. They told one another gossip, feelings about things and people. They exchanged opinions. Some of their stories were real and some of them were not. But the stories made them laugh and helped relieve all the loneliness and drudgery they were going through.

Among the six who lived in the rooming house Jamu was the only one whom Harish knew before. The two of them kind of grew up together. Jamu was the youngest among his six siblings. After he got married the brothers separated and split their parental properties. The joint family that existed until then collapsed. He could not support both him and his wife from the small piece of land he inherited. So with the help of a relative he came to Calcutta. The relative was in some kind of business. He taught his charge how to approach customers. Jamu became a quick learner, picked up all the nuances of the street vending easily. He sold flowers on the street.

Harihar was a barber. He came from a family that for generations had been cutting men's hair in his village. Harihar's father, brother, uncles and cousins continued this traditional family business. By birth, all of them fell into this profession and were obligated to cut men's hair. They collected grain at the end of the year. If there was a wedding or death in a family, they performed special services and collected fees in cash and kind. Their fortune depended on the collective fortune of the villagers they served. That is why Harihar decided to leave his village and seek his fortune in Calcutta. He felt he could make more money by doing the same outside the village, especially in a big city like Calcutta. Every day, he sat at an intersection. With his tools in hand – a pair of scissors, a blade, a nail clipper, some scented oil and a jug of water – he waited for his customers to come for a hair cut or shave. He had regular customers.

Jagannath was a farmer back home and the only son of his parents. His father left the family a few acres of land when he died. Because of the flood and drought, growing crops became an increasingly risky business. Jagannath did not mind working hard in the field but he needed a dependable income. That is how the idea of coming to Calcutta came into his mind. He thought he could do odd jobs and make some real money. Presently, he works in a shop that sells coal and firewood for cooking purposes. He splits wood there. Compared to the backbreaking work he used to do in the village, wood splitting was easy and it gave him a salary at the end of the week. Keeping the barest minimum for his maintenance, he usually sent all the money to his family.

Narayan's family had traditionally been in business. His father died when he was very young. In order to make a living, his mother used to peddle all kind of trinkets in different neighborhoods. His uncles and aunts never liked him or his mother. They thought they could get hold of his father's share of the property after his death. But his mother wouldn't let them steal it. With hard work and sheer tenacity she was able to fend them off. When Narayan was old enough to work, he did odd jobs in the village. Finally, with the help of a distant relative he came to Calcutta. Presently, he works in a restaurant as a maker of sweets. He kneads the dough, fries the cheese and makes all kind of sweet, syrupy balls. His ambition is to open his own shop some day. In order to fulfill his dreams he needs skill and money. He is trying to save enough money to open his own restaurant someday. His wife and mother live in the village. Narayan's in-laws are well off. At times of emergency they look after his wife and mother. He sends them money regularly.

Krishna comes from a milkman family. Traditionally, his family has been milking cows for generations. At home, his mother and grandmother made all kinds of cheese, curd and butter. As a boy he was expected to carry on the family tradition of taking the herd of cows into the field and bringing them back home in the evening. When he grew up he was expected to become a farmer. Nobody knows who set up these expectations. But they were there as an unwritten law. Every one just followed them. Krishna did not want to follow the traditional pattern. He left home. Without any education but with a strong desire to succeed in life he left his village. In Calcutta he managed to find a job in a jute mill. He managed to learn to write his name and read books. He is single and does not want to get married. Whatever he earns he spends at will. Krishna was the youngest in the family. Therefore every one in the rooming house treated him like a kid brother.

In the hierarchy of India's caste system Harish was on the highest rung. But here in the rooming house he was one of six people who lived there. Since the common purpose of their being in the big city was to make money to support their respective families back home, they got along with each other without difficulty. Each was very supportive of the other. They shared a common dream of improving their economic condition. Theirs was a brotherhood of the needy. Each of them had a strong realization that fate had not been favorable to them. Their birth into poverty had made life harder for them. But they seemed to be determined to face it. They also believed in fate.

In the rooming house, all six of them rarely gathered at the same time. Krishna worked on shifts. Jagannath and Narayan came home after their shops closed. And the closing of the shops depended on the volume of business the shops did. Jamu's street vending continued well into the night. Harihar left the rooming house very early in the morning and returned by late evening. Depending on where he was performing the puja, Harish returned to the rooming house at different times. If it was very late in the night his clients sent him home on a rickshaw or Tonga. The first boarder getting home cooked dinner for everyone. All of them shared the cleaning. Whenever there was a special occasion or emergency back in the village, the residents of the rooming house went to their respective villages. While there, they visited the homes of their friends to tell their loved ones that everything was fine in Calcutta. They brought back messages for the friends at the rooming house.

From the village, each of them returned with tales of sorrow and happiness. They shared their stories with each other. If it was a sad story such as the death of a child or a parent or a relative then by sharing the sorrow they got a sense of relief. If it was a story of happiness then by sharing among friends they expanded the story in their minds like hot air. Together, they all became happier.

At the work places, on the streets and in private houses Harish and his friends managed to meet with people whose lives also resembled theirs. They were all in the city to make a living.

Everyday while selling flowers on the street Jamu passed through a particular neighborhood that was well known for brothels. Clad in colorful saris, women known as "girls" looked out through open windows of their houses. They dressed in provocative styles and hauntingly invited – in a way enticed - customers to come inside. The girls wore jasmine on their breaded hair and were Jamu's regular customers. Sometimes the girls would ask Jamu to sell flowers on credit. After a few bad deals, Jamu became wise and stopped giving credit to any one in that neighborhood. The girls seemed to operate independently. But they were not free. A "Mama" controlled their every move. She was a foul mouthed, fearsome woman endowed with a big girth. The girls feared her all the time. Sometimes one of the mamas could buy half of Jamu's entire stock for the day. He came to know several mamas in the neighborhood. He also learned to treat them equally. The women in the neighborhood were seductive. But all he wanted was to sell flowers. For him the foul mouthed, heavyset mamas and the cute and seductive girls were important since they were his customers. He called each of them "sister" and he called the mama "mother". Such attribution gave those women a degree of respect they did not get from others. The women looked at Jamu like a brother or a son. For him this also created a safe relationship. The girls were from Hindu families. They performed rituals in their private lives such as fasting, puja and chanting.

At times a rich Zamindar from Bihar or a prince from some other part of the country would come to patronize the neighborhood. He and his party would scout for pretty girls. All the mamas would be on their toes and all the girls would be in their best attires. For anyone connected with a brothel this was a great event. Every mama's girl wanted to catch a prince!

Through Jamu, Harish was introduced to the community of prostitutes who needed pujas performed in their own places. They offered money and became respectful clients of Harish. The women lived an entirely different life in the morning than the night before. Sometimes it was impossible for Harish to fathom how these women switched their life style from one spectrum to another so easily! In the morning, they looked like sanyasinis – bathed, long hair hanging down their backs, a paste of sandalwood pressed to their foreheads. They wore white saris and prayed with folded hands. Harish rarely came to the neighborhood in the evening. He preferred to remember the women as he saw them in the morning. However, each of the women had a story of her own. Through deaths in the family, rejection by the community, missteps in life each of them had been dealt a bad hand in life. At times the women told their life stories to Harish. They wanted to tell someone to lessen their burdens. They told their story to Harish because he happened to be there. They trusted him.

Like the "girls" of the red light area, Harish came to know some of the laborers who lived in make shift shacks by the river. During rain the water flowed through the shacks. No one seemed to mind. The laborers kept all their possessions on a string bed where they slept. The shacks were made of thrown away materials of all kinds – a brick here, a piece of wood there, some layers of burlap bags as a roof. The shacks had a purpose but no design. After the rain, life for the residents became normal again. This was a colony of mostly men. Very few had their families with them. On special occasions they invited Harish to perform a Puja.

Like Harish, each of them had come to Calcutta to earn a few rupees and send it home so the family members could live better. By any standard they were poor. But poverty never bothered them. Their expectations were not beyond their reach. From very early in life they learned to expect much less of themselves. Therefore, they were happy by achieving whatever they got in life. The laborers in the shacks worked hard during the day; smoked hashish occasionally in the evening. Their "basti" in the city was an extension of their village life from where they came. All of them spoke the same language and ate the same kind of food. Among them and the people like them Harish felt very comfortable. Over a period of time he came to know many of them.

Harish also came to know a number of shop keepers. Occasionally he would be invited by them to perform religious ceremonies at their shops. Some of them lived nearby and owned a home in the city. He would also go to their homes. The shopkeepers were well off but suffered from all kinds of worries. They worried about their competition; they worried about being robbed; they worried about their health, their children and their future. No matter how much wealth they had they always wanted to have more and the very desire to get more kept them perennially worried.

Through Jamu, Harish came to know some of the vendors on the street who all day hawked various goods like hairpins, slates, pencils, glass bottles, pens, bath oils, combs and hundreds of other things. Some time they too needed divine intervention for the growth of their businesses. They all wanted to be big. Harish blessed their trays and carts. In return he got a salutation and some money. Those small traders worked hard. With meager capital, their businesses seemed to be always hand to mouth. They seemed to be cunning, desperate and always looking for a divine intervention of some sort. In his own way Harish wondered if he would ever be like one of them.

Harish came to know people in different parts of the city whose life styles were different from each other. Some of them were highly educated and worked for the government. Some of them were very rich who had servants and lived in big houses. Many of those rich families had estates and Zamindaries in the countryside. Others were dirt poor. The most unfortunate ones lived on the street and begged for food and money. Some of his contacts were businessmen, hawkers, prostitutes, laborers and priests. In a way his life in Calcutta was connected with many other lives that the city sheltered.

In addition to performing Puja, Harish also did palm readings. Everyone wanted to know about his or her future. Because it was unforeseeable and distant, every individual's interest lay in knowing what was ahead. The lines on one's palms were supposedly connected to one's fate and future. A lot of people believed that the way the lines formed in one's palms also determined the twists and turns of one's life. The knowledge to recognize those curves by reading the lines on the palms was a special skill. Harish was skillful in palm reading. After his father died his maternal uncle had taught him the nuances of this particular science. The hidden dots on the lines on the palm and distance between the lines and the distance between each of those hidden dots supposedly determined one's fate. Harish had studied the subject but did not believe it. Now in Calcutta he found that almost everyone he came into contact with was interested in knowing his or her future. Each of them wanted to know what was stored in their palms for them. Getting out of the grinding of the present was a passion that everyone seemed to have. The present consisted of struggles and problems. They needed an escape from it. In Harish's expertise in knowing the future they saw an indication of changing the course of their oppressive present.

In addition to palm reading Harish also started reading and preparing horoscopes. One has to know certain mathematical formulas to determine some one's fortune by reading his/her horoscope. The positions of sun, moon and planets and their mutual relationships to each other at the time of one's birth supposedly determined one's entire road map for life. As the heavenly powers moved from place to place, according to this science, they changed one's fortune on earth. At times, their positions revealed their anger. At other times, their positions meant they were ready to help. Since fortunes were made and destroyed by powers that be in the heavens, the people living in Calcutta had little control over it. They did not have to take the blame for their actions or lack of it. Once again it was an easy escape for many from their oppressive present. By blaming the stars they could easily dodge accountability.

A displeased, ill-placed or ill-tempered planet in one's horoscope needed proper worshipping for its pacification. Sometimes the process required chanting a particular Vedic mantra a thousand times or the offering of one thousand basil leaves to a particular God or Goddess. All the planets and stars were symbolized in the form of a round pebble, a piece of black granite. Very carefully Harish carried this precious pebble in his bag. For whatever planet or star he was to worship on behalf of a client he used this black granite as the symbol. Like a doctor determining an illness Harish learned to tell people their fortunes by calculating the positions of stars and planets by reading their horoscopes. He was confident in telling the ebb and flow of their fortunes by reading their palms. He sympathized with those whose fortunes were at a low point. He expressed happiness for those who were riding high.

Every disease has its cure. The same way, every misfortune caused by heavenly powers also has its remedy. Whenever Harish mentioned bad luck caused by the configuration of heavenly powers, he prescribed an antidote for it. Most of the time, he prescribed a puja or chanting. Those who had problems in life or faced a serious crisis thought that such a thing was happening to them because of bad luck. Somewhere some God or Goddess must be angry with them. Therefore they needed to pacify the deity. Harish's suggestions tied into their fears and feelings. Through him they saw a way out. If things were going well, then the happy individual was thankful for good luck. He/ she wanted to express his or her gratitude by offering a puja performed by Harish. Their intention was to keep things unchanged. In a very practical way this brought him new business and income. In a strange way, some of Harish's clients saw that he had a special relationship with the deities he worshipped. They liked it. Therefore, whatever he asked as his fee they did not mind. They found him to be rather inexpensive. Besides, performing a puja in one's own home instead of doing it in a temple was convenient.

Slowly and slowly Harish became a man of Calcutta rather than of his village. Yes, his roots lay in the village. But as time went on he planted his feet more and more into the city. At times he missed his village. But he was happy to be in Calcutta because it provided him with a good income. He liked the people he hobnobbed with. People of Calcutta, compared to those in the village, looked more sophisticated and cleaner. Every one's life followed a routine or pattern. The milkman came to the neighborhood with his milk in the morning. The newspaper man hawked his newspaper. The fruit vendor brought his pushcart through the street; the fisherman opened his stall on the street corner; the markets opened as well as closed; people ran toward the train station to go places; office workers and dock workers went to their jobs. All of them followed a schedule. There was regularity and predictability in all of this.

Because so many people lived in a city like Calcutta their problems spilled over to their surroundings. The atmosphere often appeared to be chaotic. Hundreds of people passed through the street. Yet, hardly did any one know the other. They seemed to be afraid of each other. Their enormous numbers created fear for them as if they were afraid of their own shadow. It was excruciating as well as exciting. Harish loved the excitement. He did not mind the Calcutta life. He got used to it. After weeks, months and years he became one of the multitudes he saw everyday.

About two or three times a year Harish went home to his village. He took with him bags of good things impossible to get in the village, such as raisins, soaps, candles etc. The serenity of the village and the company of his wife, daughter and mother always energized him. The distance had created a special fondness between him and Haru. Every time he went home he felt as if he was falling in love with her all over again. It was exciting to see Sudha's growth in inches and in ideas. She was slowly turning into a beautiful young lady, a poem in flesh and blood. On the other hand his mother was growing feebler. Out of concern he would suggest "Mother, you should take better care of yourself."

"How long do you think I am going to live? What is the use of keeping this useless body, any way" his mother would reply.

He knew that his mother could not be persuaded to change

her ways. She was stubborn to the core. Harish was worried for his mother and his worries reflected in Haru's thinking. "I will take care of her. You should not keep worrying about everybody. Mother looks thin. But she is fine." Haru's consoling voice would abate his concern. He could trust Haru.

Every time Harish returned from the village he would immediately write home that he got to Calcutta safely. And then he would wait for Haru's reply. Both of them wanted a son. "Sudha is getting spoiled because she has no one to share her toys with. She needs a brother" – he would remember his mother's comment

Every time he returned to Calcutta from home, Harish waited for Haru's letter to tell him that she was pregnant. If it really happened, the news of her pregnancy would lift his spirist. He would hope for a male child and pray. Like Haru he prayed for a son everyday. Harish would be concerned for Haru's condition. He knew that his mother would give her proper advice and care. Then again in another letter in a few months the bad news would come. And he would be upset for days and weeks.

In Haru's case biology plaid a trick. She had two miscarriages. The news was always a blow to him. He would be silently crying for his shattered hopes. Harish would imagine Haru's grief stricken face. He would wish to be there with her. All the time he would be mourning the child that never was.

Harish calculated the placement of his and his wife's stars. It appeared to him that all the stars were settled in favorable positions. He attributed Haru's miscarriage to their bad luck. He theorized that the deity in the temple in his village was not being cared for properly. That is why the deity might be angry with them. He suggested that Haru offer milk to the deity every Monday which she obediently did.

After two consecutive miscarriages Haru had developed a kind of cynicism toward the fairness of Gods and Goddesses. She was in a mood to strangle any one of them if she could only see them. Her wounded heart spewed anger toward heavenly powers. She was angry with the Gods.

After each miscarriage and shattered hope that came with it, her misery continued from days to weeks. In a time like this, Jhumpi was careful not to give her too much advice. She knew that the grief that had engulfed Haru's heart was like a wild fire. She wanted it to burn itself out so that the new growth could eventually take place. Haru would cry for days. And then the tears would dry up. She would begin to snap out of her loss. Slowly, she would emerge from her stupor. With a big scar in the core of her heart she would return to life but the scar would never go away. Many miles away in Calcutta Harish would feel the same loss and pain. In their own ways both would continue to deal with life as it presented itself.

Years went by. Haru and Harish's lives passed through many hopes and disappointments. Materially speaking, Harish became well off. He rebuilt his broken house. With rupees earned in Calcutta he was able to buy a patch of land in the village. By any standard he was not a rich man. But in his village he became known as a well off man. Harish's financial strength pleased Jhumpi to no end. All of her life she had lived from hand to mouth. Now that Harish was way above that it made her very happy. She felt the need for one thing that her son had not given her yet. For the continuity of the family tree she wanted a grandson. She loved Sudha. But she knew one day Sudha would be someone else's daughter in law. It is the son who stayed within the family. Therefore, she wanted a grandson - her son's son. She prayed a lot to have her wish fulfilled. For a long time it did not happen.

Sudha was about 11 years old when Haru finally gave birth to a son. The boy seemed to be healthy and always hungry. Given the history of Haru's miscarriages, it was a miracle that the child was born as a full term baby. Every one in the family thought it was a miracle. Harish ran from Calcutta to see his newborn son. He brought toys for the child. In the village he observed a special puja for his son. He contributed one hundred coconuts to the temple and worshipped the deity in the village for his blessing.

9

As a child and then up to a point in his youth Harish had enjoyed his life in the village. Its open space, the changing scenery in different seasons, water flowing in the river, cattle grazing in the field and crops waiting to be harvested in the fields had been a part of his growing up. However, after living in Calcutta for years he came to realize that he could no longer be able to live in his village. For him, over the years, the village became an increasingly awkward place. He began to loath muddy roads and the devastating floods followed by diseases like cholera and smallpox. Yet his attraction for his village bordered on romanticism. He loved its simplicity. In a way he was attached to his village and was always willing to forgive its shortcomings.

In the village his old friends, like him, were getting older. Those with whom he had played in the fields, swum in the river or argued about stupid things just for the sake of argument had developed gray hair like him. Some of them had gone completely bald. Family problems involving children and aging parents were the issues that took most of their attention. They seemed to be overwhelmed. Health was another problem. As his friends became older they developed ailments - some of them chronic. Since there was no doctor in the area, finding the exact reasons for their ailments was impossible. The medicine men guessed their diseases and prescribed various roots and leaves. In a very speculative way they did the treatment. With prayer and faith the sick took the medicine. Some were cured and some were not. Those who did not get better blamed their destiny and waited for the final result. Harish did not have to go through the same difficulties. He was relatively healthy. Some of his old friends were happy for him. Others were jealous because he escaped their fate. Harish appeared to be neither happy nor sad. He loved the village and missed it in Calcutta. At the same time he was so used to being in a big city that he began missing it after a few days in the village. Other than having a cold or headache now and then he enjoyed his good health and good fortune.

Because of his relative affluence his neighbors and relatives developed a certain expectation of him. The expectation consisted mostly of financial help. He was affluent but not wealthy. In view of the needs of his relatives and neighbors he did not have enough. Yet, that did not prevent them from asking for help. At the time of need the relatives seemed to have a different persona. They were full of friendliness. He tried to help them as much as he could. As soon as their problems were over, they seemed to have completely forgotten their predicaments of the past and the help they got from Harish. In several cases he found that those whom he helped did not even want to remember the incident. If money was involved, he tried to collect but most of the time his efforts were unsuccessful.

Such experiences became lessons for him. Those who were ungrateful he stayed away from them. Those who were grateful he did not mind helping again. Regardless of what happened at the individual level between him and the other person, they both had their roots in the village. Harish lived in Calcutta whereas his mother and wife and children stayed in the village. At the time of a dire need, his family had to depend on the people of the village. Therefore, helping others was a kind of insurance for him.

Over the years, a lot of new faces had appeared in the village. The sons and nephews of his friends were young men now. Little girls who used to climb on his shoulder, were now getting ready to leave for their in-laws' houses as young brides. Harish also saw the passing of older people. Haru's parents used to be a great support but within a period of two years both of them died. It made Haru very sad.

The village consisted of many joint families where parents, uncles, aunts, cousins and brothers lived together as individual parts of an extended family under the same roof. The village lacked school, health care facility and roads. Yet, nobody seemed to miss them because those who lived in the village never had them. Those who had been to a big city like Calcutta had seen paved roads and hospitals and schools. They knew that the needs for such things existed. Their way of thinking began to influence others and slowly the entire village seemed to need things that it never had. A wave of rising expectations took place.

Harish, now a middle- aged man of means, had seen his own expectations rise. He hoped that one day his son would attend a high school in the nearby town. Having a high school in his village was possible but unthinkable at this time. He imagined himself to be a proud father of a young man with a government job that he never had. A job in the government brought prestige and money. Above all else it opened up avenues for many good things in life. He wanted his son to have them. The things that he aspired but never could achieve - a house in the nearby town, several more acres of land, a brick house in the village and many new ornaments of gold for Haru. In the eyes of many of his neighbors he had wealth. They had much less than he had. The old timers in the village knew how poor he was while growing up. On seeing him better off, they felt happy and proud of his achievements. In many ways they looked up to him. Yet, in Harish's own mind he had very little compared to those he saw at Calcutta.,

In Calcutta Harish had seen how the rich families lived. They had palatial houses; the kind of affluence they enjoyed was mind-boggling. Many of those families were born into wealth. Harish knew that he was born into poverty. Therefore, he was convinced that he could never reach their level. That is why no matter what others in the village thought of him, he could never think of himself as a rich man. Compared to many others in the village he may have been a bit better off. But in his own mind he was never a rich man. He wanted his son Anand to be really prosperous when he grew up. He wanted his daughter Sudha to marry the son of a very wealthy man. He desired to achieve all the unfulfilled dreams of his life through his children.

Whenever Harish returned to his village he spent considerable time in motivating his son Anand to go to school regularly. Anand seemed to be a child totally oblivious to the needs or demands of the world. Like any child of his age he lived in a universe of his own and was loved by everyone around him. His mother and grandmother hardly let him go out of their sight. His sister loved him and like any other older sister taught him how to survive in the world by not putting his hand in a burning fire or not going too close to the cow when it was nursing its calf. He loved eating sweet things. For him his grandmother had made special arrangements with a farmer to provide bananas regularly.

Someone in the village was engaged in bee keeping. The grandmother bought honey from him by the jars. Whenever the little boy did any mischief, he was threatened that he would be reported to his father. In this way Anand developed a special respect and fear of his father. Whenever Harish returned home from Calcutta, the little boy was ready to show him what a good child he was. Through letters from home Harish knew everything about his son's behavior. Haru always gave a vivid description of his mischief. Whenever he got a letter from her, Harish read and reread it from top to bottom. The letter represented the faces of Haru and the children. Its very presence lifted his spirit.

Because of his work in Calcutta he could not visit his family as much as he wanted to. It was expensive and he could not afford so many travels. Still he visited his family three or four times a year. Depending on the season, he stayed in the village one to three weeks. Whenever he announced the day of his departure, Haru would always ask him when he was coming back the next time. He would answer in an evasive way. His mother would always remind him that she was getting older by the hour and wouldn't be able to see him again in her life time.

"You will be alright mother" Harish would reply.

Now Sudha was growing up fast. She would look upset at the departure of her father. But it was Anand who would cling to him like Sudha used to when she was a little girl. Momentarily, Harish would feel torn between his commitment to making a living in a faraway place and his attachment to his family in the village. Even if outwardly he appeared resolute and strong he would leave the village as an emotional wreck. It was always difficult for him to leave. It would take him a few days to get used to Calcutta again. Just the same way, coming from Calcutta took him a few days to adjust to his village. But the experience and the emotions were different.

Over the years, Harish became adept displaying two different kinds of personalities. In the city he was a man who hobnobbed with sophisticated wealthy men and talked in polished language. He wore clean clothes and had sandals on his feet. He never asked his clients about their caste. Since moneymaking was the driving force behind all his activities, any consideration that stood in its way had to be discarded. Therefore, he could read anyone's palm or make an astrological chart for any one who was willing to pay him. In a restaurant he could accept tea from the hand of any server who worked there. The server could be a Muslim, an" untouchable" or a Brahmin. He could be seen talking to prostitutes in their houses or to working women on the street. Nobody would be surprised or think of it out of place. In many ways Calcutta was different. It was a city where people of different backgrounds got together because of their respective needs. There, all of them, in tens of thousands, seemed to be focused on making a living. Harish was just one of them. But the village was different. It was traditional. The line between dos and don'ts was rigid and substantial. No one living there could cross it. When he was in the village he could not wear sandals while crossing the sidewalks of the temple. Talking to any woman on the street was taboo unless the woman was his mother or sister or a close relative. Each individual in the village belonged to a particular caste and one's position – regardless of wealth – was determined by birth. By virtue of being born, everyone in the village was stuck in a cocoon, a predetermined position or so it seemed. The village never gave any one a chance to get out of this cocoon. One had to break away to declare one's individual identity.

For a villager, it was easy to live the life that had been going on for ages. Harish was uncomfortable with many of its rules. As a man living in the village he could not undo any of these rules all by himself. Those who benefited from these outmoded social prescriptions were eager to guard its elements at any cost. Therefore, no one in his right mind wanted to behave differently. If Harish wanted to break any of the rules he had to fight with a whole lot of people. It would have been ugly and dangerous for him and his family. He lacked courage to change the rules. He honored the caste system and took his rightful place in its hierarchy. Like others in the village he did not want to make waves. Yet, those who remained at the receiving end of social injustice seemed to be making waves. Their stirring bred conflict. And the news of this conflict was being heard at different places, in villages and in towns. The news of conflicts came through newspapers that he seldom read as he was too engrossed in his own problems. In Calcutta he always waited for a letter from home. If it was good he became happy. If it was not then he got worried and prayed for its resolution. In the village he always felt that he was there only for a few days.

.It was not at all difficult for Harish to move his positions back and forth. By living in the big city he developed a somewhat cosmopolitan outlook about things and people. In the village, he became a conformist whom the outmoded social stratification did not bother. Like many of his generation, he was conditioned to think in certain ways because he was born into a village society. Only the escape from its parameters to a big city where no one knew him liberated his thoughts. Like millions of his fellow citizens he saw no inconsistency in his mental shift from one place to another.

The last time, like any other time, when Harish left his village for Calcutta, Haru looked sad. She seemed to be reluctant to let him go. There was a special sadness about her. In order to avoid his own thoughts he told her aloud "Don't worry. As soon as I get to Calcutta I will write to you". Haru knew he would.

Once Harish reached Calcutta, he got busy with ever so many things. Yet he did not forget to write to his wife. While writing his letter he could feel the touch of Anand on his back. He could feel the curious look in Sudha's eyes around him and the happy face of Haru. A strong emotion would engulf him. "This is the price of making a living" he would console himself.

Throughout his years in Calcutta he had never received a letter from Haru where she had complained about anything. Never had she mentioned her own illness. She always wrote about his mother, about neighbors and about the children; hardly anything was mentioned about her. When coming home for a few days or a few weeks, he would learn that Haru had been sick or she had a bad headache during such and such puja or she collapsed on such an occasion. He would be upset. "You should have let me know" he would tell his wife in mock anger.

"I am okay. You are making too much fuss about my health" – Haru would protest

Around Harish, she showed confidence and downplayed problems relating to her health. Whenever the issue of her health came up she would say, "I am as healthy as a horse". Harish adored her. She knew it. He was proud of her. Whenever he talked to others about his wife, his voice filled with emotion. His words invariably carried love and affection for her.

Haru was a devoted mother. Both Sudha and Anand loved her dearly. Yet, she was stern with them and kept an eye on them at all times. Harish felt reassured that Haru was such a capable woman, a perfect mother for his children. He knew that his own mother was sometimes difficult to deal with. Once she was convinced that she was right, hardly did anything matter to her. Haru knew how to handle her. He trusted Haru's judgment. Even if he had a great deal of love for his mother it was Haru's judgment that he trusted most. And trusting her judgment was convenient as it spared him of making a decision critical or not.

On her part, Haru was devoted to her family. In her husband's absence from home she managed all of the affairs of the household. She cooked and cleaned and took care of the pets. If anything needed repaired she sent for the repairman. In a very regular basis she let Harish know what was happening in the village and at home. So he was very much aware of all the happenings in his village and his family. Haru was always careful to mention her mother- in - law's health. As she grew older, the mother in law kept complaining about her aching joints and strained back muscles. Haru was very careful not to let her strain her back for anything. But it was not easy. The elderly woman was very independent minded and did exactly what she wanted to do regardless who said what. Yet, Haru's suggestive way of speaking had some impact on her and more often than not she listened to her daughter-in- law. Every evening Haru made it a point to massage her mother- in- law's feet before going to bed. Now that Sudha was a big girl she did this job with a great deal of enthusiasm. Sudha often wondered about her grandmother's hanging skin and thin bony legs. "Grandma has the legs of a stork" she would chuckle.

Haru would explain to her in a positive way" when people get older they lose muscles. This is why grandma's legs look thin and her skin is sagging. A long time ago grandma was young like you. She was beautiful"

In the last couple of visits home Harish became convinced that Haru had been working very hard and that over the years, she had been tackling all the problems at home while he had been away. As a result his attraction for her increased skyward. But he felt her health has deteriorated considerably and she had been very discreet about it. Harish felt bad. It occurred to him that all the men who have left the village to make a living outside have put their wives through the same grind. Because of the help from their wives the men have been able to survive in distant places. The men knew that while each of them was busy making a living, the wife in the village was looking after the children and the house. In a collective way they enjoyed a sense of stability. And stability gave them hope.

Harish often wondered how his life would have been without a wife like Haru. She was everything a man needed in a woman. She could read and write. She could cook very well and she was beautiful. Her soothing voice was the most beautiful thing he had ever heard. Above all else she had a wonderful personality that was the combination of all of the above. She did not like to confront anyone. Whenever she found herself in a confrontational situation she just walked away even if she was right. "You don't attain God by argument" she would quote from a well- used proverb. In Harish's way of thinking this was not a good philosophy. But Haru had her own way of solving problems. Her solution matched her personality. In his own way he was proud of her.

One day Harish was getting ready to go to a client's house, the mailman arrived at his door. Usually the mailman came around noon. But it was not even nine o' clock yet. "He must be in a hurry" he assumed.

"Is Harish Mishra here?" asked the mailman.

"I am Harish Mishra". Harish said.

"I have a telegram for you" told the mailman. After making him sign a piece of paper the mailman handed him the telegram that read WIFE SERIOUS. COME HOME. MOTHER

Harish felt as if the ground split under his feet. Momentarily, he felt numb and stunned. All kinds of fearful thoughts raced through his head. He knew he had to board the next train toward the village. Reaching the village required a ten hour journey by train followed by half a day of walking. Harish became homeward bound within hours.

On the way, everything seemed to pass by him like an unreal dream. He saw the objects. He felt many of them. Yet, he was unable to realize what those objects were or meant to him. His mind was focused on the thought of Haru's health. Nothing seemed to matter much at the moment. He bought the ticket and boarded the train. The train on its way stopped at different stations. Crowds of people entered and disembarked. The hawkers at each station and inside the compartment hawked their peanuts, tea, pakoras and much more as they always did. Harish did not buy anything and did not want anything. Hours later he got to his destination. The train station was a cement floor with a tin roof. A few vendors and a handful of beggars mingled in the place. A black milk-cow grazed lazily in a distance. It seemed to be an isolated place – almost nowhere. Harish wished there were someone in the train station whom he knew and whom he could ask about Haru. But he did not know anyone there. So he kept walking. It was daybreak and he knew it would be afternoon before he reached the village.

The summer breeze in the morning felt soothing. Before the sun became really hot he paced himself faster. The familiar tree where he used to rest on his way to the train station; the sweet shop half way to his village where he used to drink water and buy a glass of curd were all there. But their existence did not matter to him today. He just kept passing them. He was worried. He did not want to stop. He did not feel like stopping anywhere. But he was thirsty. He found a well on the roadside. Harish drew water from the well with a tin can attached to a rope that was there. He drank heartily. Then he splashed some cold water on his face and wetted his head. It made him feel somewhat stronger and once again he kept walking. Going into his village meant crossing a couple of small streams and a river and farm lands. In the hot sun the sand on the river bed was hot. His bare feet almost blistered. Yet, Harish did not mind and did not care about those minor inconveniences. That was the reality of going to the village. The only thing that was in his mind now was Haru's health.

In the afternoon Harish reached the outskirts of the village. A fisherman was returning home with his catches. Recognizing Harish from a distance he tried to strike up a conversation "Sister-in- law is ill. I guess you got the telegram yesterday". The fisherman referred to Haru as "sisetr- in- law". In the village everyone is some way was related to everyone. The fisherman was no exception. The way the man talked it assured Harish that Haru was still living. But "would she still be alive when I reach home? Would she still be able to recognize me? What led to her ailment?" – Numerous thoughts popped into his mind. He found no answer to any of his own questions, Harish felt headache and tried to stop thinking. He got worried. Yet, for the sake of civility he kept talking to the fisherman who offered to carry the bundle he had on his shoulder. Harish thanked the man for his gesture.

When he reached home he could not believe what he saw. Haru was lying on the bed in their room. She could not muster any strength to get up to greet him. She looked like a skeleton. Her hair was unkempt. Her face sank to a depth Harish had never seen. Yet, she instinctively felt his presence in the room. Her face lit up in spite of her illness. Her eyes welled up in tears. Haru tried to get up and do things for him. But she was too weak to do so. Her inability to get up made her embarrassed. Looking straight into her husband's eyes she said in a very low voice "you must be tired". She knew that as soon as Harish got the telegram he left Calcutta.

Now that she was ill, she did not know what was ahead of her. She was concerned about the children. She was worried about her husband. She did not know what would happen to all of them. Her thoughts resonated in Harish's mind also. He did not know how they would manage without her. He felt like crying. Had it been any other time she would have been instantly running around to do things for him. She would have been opening his bag to distribute gifts for the children. She would have been asking about the trip, his roommates. Today Harish missed all of that. Memories from the past overwhelmed him. "How are you feeling?" He asked Haru. In his heart he prayed for her recovery. She could hardly answer any of his questions.

Harish, sitting by her, ran his fingers through her hair. His fingers running through her black hair created a vibration in his body and mind that gave him warmth and strength. At the moment his only wish was for Haru to get better. Harish wanted his life to continue smoothly. He dreaded the future without Haru and the disruption it would breed. Haru's eyes were closed. She sensed the tender and loving touch of Harish's hand. But she was too tired physically and emotionally. Tears rolled down her cheeks. She took Harish's hand in hers. "I don't think I can make it" – she said in a whisper.

"You will be alright. I will call the medicine man. He will cure you." Harish tried to cheer her up.

"Medicine is going to do no good. Why waste money? I feel I am dying. It is good that you are here."

"Don't talk like that" Harish protested.

Three months ago when Harish came home Haru looked different and now she is not herself anymore. Before Haru became ill she had serious bleeding for days. By then she was pregnant. In one of her letters to him she had given a hint of her pregnancy. She was looking forward to delivering their third child. For reasons unknown to her she had a miscarriage. The fetus died. She blamed herself for the miscarriage. It made her sad and remorseful. In her own mind she accused herself for her baby's death. "It must be the result of sins from my previous life" she reasoned.

Bleeding made her physically weak and brought on other complications. Yet, it was the mental anguish that made her so ill. At this point she did not want to get better. In her heart she wanted to a-tone the death of her fetus by dying herself. She was emotionally devastated and physically ruined. She lost her appetite along with her zeal to fight to continue living. Sudha would bring her a glass of lemonade. She would take a sip and then put down the glass. Jhumpi would encourage her to eat something like vegetable broth or puffed-rice. She and Sudha would bring a bowl of food to her. But she would refuse to eat. Haru's condition made the older woman nervous. Now that her son was in the village she felt better.

Upon his arrival, Harish encouraged Haru to put something in her stomach. He had brought a couple of apples from Calcutta. He peeled the skin of one and cut it into small pieces. Then he encouraged her to eat them. Harish's prodding worked but she was too weak to lift her fingers. Harish fed her the cut apple piece by piece. Haru managed to eat a few pieces until she couldn't eat any more. So she asked him to give the rest to Anand.

The boy was genuinely scared about his mother lying on the bed. Sudha, a teenager now, could tolerate her mother's illness with a sense of understanding. But for Anand all of this was strange. He had never seen his mother lying in bed like this – crying and looking sad. The situation was very difficult for him. Sudha loved her brother and most of the time Anand clung to her like a monkey on a branch. Since the day their mother fell ill she would try to distract Anand's fear and concerns in different ways. She knew that their grandmother was too old and fragile to deal with Anand's robust playfulness. Besides, their grandmother had to deal with all the problems that appeared at hand,

Sudha was happy that her father was home now. Even if he was sad and overwhelmed, his presence in the house gave everybody strength and confidence. There were chores in the house like cooking, cleaning and feeding the cow that needed to be done. Like her father and grandmother she was also sad for her mother's illness. She missed her solid presence and engaging hands around the house. But Sudha was old enough to act responsibly. In a very short time she had to grow up quite a bit.

She had to learn to act like a grown up girl. In her mother's convalescence she had to take charge. Now, she became a child adult. She realized that her father and grandmother depended on her and her brother needed her.

10

Harish was not prepared for this and no one was. A little before the daybreak Haru's head slumped on the pillow. She was gone. Prior to dying she was ill, very ill. It was frightening for Harish to see her that way. From the beginning, the moment he heard about it, he was apprehensive about her health. But he had hoped that she would get better eventually. Throughout their married years she had never complained about her health.

Harish called in the best medicine man in his area living a few villages away. The man had treated many sick people and was well known for his accurate diagnosis of diseases known and unknown. After taking medicine from him Haru seemed to feel better. In his own mind, Harish thought that she had turned the corner. He prayed for Haru's quick recovery. He sat by her. Every night he stayed awake and tended to her. Occasionally, he caressed her hair that lay scattered all over the pillow. He massaged her arms and back. Her skin felt cold and she lay on the bed utterly tired and often unable to respond to Harish' hand. In better times, she would have been responsive, self conscious and shy. With his touch on her skin she would have said in mock anger "Oh stop it, I feel goose bumps all over." She would have laughed. They both would have laughed. But now such laughter seemed to have happened eons ago. She lay on the bed ill and Harish could only wish that she get better.

For a few days Haru's condition fluctuated between getting a little better and getting a lot worse. When she seemed to be getting better, Harish's hope reached a new high. When she relapsed and felt sicker, utter hopelessness took possession of him. While giving medicine, feeding vegetable broth and helping her to drink the liquid Harish kept on playing back all the things they had done together throughout their married years . It was unthinkable for him to imagine life without her. He needed Haru to get better. He prayed to all the Gods and Goddesses for her recovery and in his prayers sought heavenly intervention for her good health that was absolutely tied to the welfare of his two children. He cared less about himself now. But he wanted Haru to live for the children. He could not imagine his children without a mother.

Like many other times in his life, the heavenly intervention did not come. Throughout the night Harish was awake by her side. His mother was dosing off nearby while holding Anand on her lap, sleeping. Poor Sudha did not know what to do. She too was half- awake. The whole family was in pins and needles all night. Hoping against hope, they all wanted Haru to get better while she lay on her bed in a state of delirium. Now and then she said something in a very feeble and incomprehensible voice. When Harish tried to understand what she said or tried to respond by asking what she wanted she would be gone. Once again she would relapse into utter silence and delirium. The children wanted their mother. Harish wanted his life to be on track again. Every one of them wanted Haru to live. But that was not to be.

When Harish saw Haru's slumped head on the pillow, his

heart sank. A horror passed through his body and soul. He called out her name. "Haru. My Haru". There was no response. Haru's eyes were closed; she had stopped breathing. Death stared from her hallowed face. She was gone. Harish let out a scream and dropped his head on the blanket that covered Haru's body. He touched her cheeks and forehead. Haru's lifeless body felt awfully cold. His scream woke up everybody. Every one wept and sobbed. By daybreak everyone in the village knew that Haru passed away.

According to the Hindu ritual one's dead body was not supposed to wait long to be cremated. So the men from the neighborhood immediately made arrangements to remove Haru's body from home. Harish was in no state of mind to do anything. The woman who gave him so much love and two wonderful children, lay dead and was to be cremated. He could not bear the thought of it. He felt a jolt of grief in his spine. Emotionally he was numb. Like him, his mother also was heartbroken. She wanted to die before anybody younger than she. But now that her daughter- in- law was gone, she genuinely asked whether God was ever fair to anyone. She wondered with all seriousness as to why God spared her and took Haru away who was so young and so much needed. But there was no reply.

Sudha faced the enormity of her mother's death. She knew for more than a month that her mother was ill and had always hoped in her heart that she would get better. She had been managing all the things that had to be managed. She had thought that the illness of her mother was temporary. It had never crossed Sudha's young mind that her mother could die. In her little world such a thing had never taken shape. Therefore, Haru's death fell up on her suddenly and with a terrible shock. It hit her like lightening from the sky. She wept for her mother and cried aloud. None of that could bring her mother back. Sick to her stomach she became terribly sad.

Anand's situation was totally different. He was bewildered. For him, someone told him, his mother's death meant that she wasn't coming back. She would no longer wipe his back with the apron of her Sari. He wouldn't be able to call "Mommy". He had no clear idea about death itself. But he knew what it meant not to have his mother. Everyone around him was sad. His father, his sister and his grandmother – each one of them looked sad, very sad. They were weeping and their sadness reflected on the young boy's heart and soul. He cried for his mother. He wanted to hide his face under her arms. He wanted to be held by his mother. She always held him even when she was very ill. But none of that was happening now. He had no concrete concept of death and kept on crying uncontrollably.

Just before the body was taken away, one of the women of the neighborhood took Anand away. For a young child to see a dead body was not good, especially if the body was of his mother. There was no use trying to console him as this was not to be the last time the boy would miss his mother. They let him cry. There was sadness all around and everyone in the neighborhood seemed to be crying. Haru was so well liked by so many. Her death seemed to touch everyone who knew her. Exhausted from crying so hard, Anand in the midmorning fell asleep on a straw mat.

As the custom dictated, four men from the neighborhood carried Haru's body to the cemetery. Harish walked in front of them spreading petals of flower, rice and miniature conch shells. According to the long held belief among villagers, especially women, a woman is lucky if she died before her husband did. But a widow is allotted no such luck. Haru died a married woman whose husband was still living. Therefore, she deserved special treatment. Putting flowers on the path of her last journey was one such thing. Yet, Harish was heartbroken and did not share the belief of others. He realized a long time ago that he needed Haru much more than she needed him. Without Haru, he knew he would be lost. Angry that he had to face life alone, he resented her death.

At the cemetery, with recitation from various holy books of Sanskrit, Haru's body was placed on a pile of sandalwood. Harish saw his wife's pale and ashen face for the last time and broke down.

Consoled by others he controlled himself and lit the pyre. Slowly, fire engulfed the body. For a brief moment the dead woman's face reflected through the burning fire. Then it was only fire. One could smell the burning flesh and hear the crackling of wood and burning bones. The amber of the burning fire destroyed everything. By the time the flame was gone, leaving only ashes, Haru had become a memory forever. She was no more!

After the fire died down, the pallbearers went to dip in the river. Harish brought home Haru's ash in an urn. For the next ten days, special puja had to be offered to the urn that contained the ash of Haru's body. And finally, on the tenth day, a communal mourning took place. The final observance took place on the eleventh day culminating in a communal dinner. Since Harish had lit the pyre, he was not able to cross the river or pass the boundary of the temple, as the custom demanded, until the eleventh day of the funeral. Therefore, neighbors helped him in making arrangements for all the things that needed to be done; marketing for the communal dinner, informing the relatives, keeping an eye on Anand etc. Haru's two brothers helped a great deal and Haru's sister's husband was very valuable in putting things together. He offered to take Anand to his house so the child could live in the care of his loving aunt. But Harish was in no state of mind to make a decision about anything. He just listened and did not say anything.

Relatives from different villages kept coming to the house. They remembered things about Haru and told their stories to each other. They expressed feelings of sadness and concerns for his family. All of them were caring, concerned and genuinely sad at Haru's death. "She was so young and died so suddenly" they would say. The women wept at Haru's absence and Harish felt like crying with them. But for the sake of his children he kept his emotions and his sadness bottled up in his own heart. He did not cry. But as his lips stiffened he looked away from them. The relatives were full of ideas for Harish to follow. Their views often contradicted each other. Yet, the relatives seemed to have good intentions and their presence was helpful. In a sea of sadness Harish,while feeling utterly weak and vulnerable, gained some strength from their presence. After the eleventh day of mourning, the relatives began to leave. They had their own worlds to care about and they left singly or in pairs. In a few days all of them were gone – even Haru's brothers. Their families waited for them. Harish could not expect them to stay with him to care for him and his family.

After the relatives left, the situation sank into his mind more deeply and abruptly. The house without Haru felt like an empty shell. She had painted murals on the exterior of the front wall of the house. Her saris hung from the hangers in the bedroom. Her personal care things, a bottle of nail polish, a small box of red dots, a jar of face cream, a buffalo-bone comb lay scattered here and there. For Harish, each of those objects carried memories. The very sight of each of those objects brought Haru alive. Without her physical presence, his life felt very empty now! He seemed to be at a loss to face reality. When Haru was ill, he was spending his time by caring for her in the hope that one day she would get better. By caring for her, he kept his mind away from being overwhelmed because he had something on hand to do. Her death brought all of that to an abrupt end. But he was not ready for the ending. The void created by Haru's death was unthinkable for him. Like a man drifting in the sea, he became hopeless. Yet, he could not afford to drown in despair. For the sake of his children, he had to muster strength to go on in life. However, it was easier said than done. In his own mind Harish could understand his situation. Like a man drowning in deep water he could not bring all his faculties to play at the same time.

Both Anand and Sudha missed their mother. One could see them silently crying for her. The sadness written on their faces told of their inner misery and for Harish, this was the most difficult situation to face.

Sadness was written all over Harish's face. Since Haru's untimely death he continued to live on an emotional roller coaster. Outwardly, he ate, slept and did the necessary chores around the house. He talked to his children and neighbors and took long walks aimlessly. He did all of that in a ritualistic way. One could easily see that his mind was in someplace else as if he was in big trouble and did not know how to get out of it. Haru's death was a final thing and there was no chance for improvement or change in it. He knew, she would never come back. Yet, he missed her day and night. His longing for her pushed him deeper into a sadness that showed in his actions and mood.

His mother seemed to be more sad for being left behind than the death of Haru. When nobody was around, especially to avoid her grandchildren to see her cry, his mother would wipe her wet eyes discreetly so no one would know she was crying. The situation broke his heart.

The mother knew her son's sadness. She knew how much Haru and Harish loved each other. The mother's entire world, her life, circled around Harish. For her, his present sadness became intolerable. She remembered losing her husband when she was young. She did not know then how she was going to manage with two children. She had always believed that it takes a man to feed and clothe a family. But here she was alone with two young children. Somehow she managed and God helped her. Ever since his father's death, Harish has remained the apple of her eye and the only man in her wretched life of a widow. She prayed for Harish.

All of a sudden Jhumpi felt old and ancient and helpless. "Prayer is the only thing I can do" she thought and the thought of prayer gave her inner peace. Jhumpi had never thought of herself as a religious person. Yet, she prayed. As if out of necessity! Her praying could not eliminate all the sadness from her life. She was sad at Haru's death. She was sad for Harish's sadness. She was utterly sad for her grandchildren who lost their mother so early in life. Her entire life at the moment seemed to exist like a bad dream full of sadness and sorrow. In her life, Jhumpi had endured a lot of pain and sad experiences. But Haru's death was too much for her to bear. She wished to die but could not.

One evening, when Harish was taking his evening meal Jhumpi as usual sat down in front of him. Every mother wants her son to eat with complete satisfaction. Therefore in the villages of India mothers sit and guide their sons to be a good eater. This is a ritual all village women perform religiously. It is a habit that is handed from generation to generation. Young or old, all the mothers in the village observe this practice. For Jhumpi, this was a practice very familiar and very ordinary. While eating, the person also becomes a captive listener. Therefore, all the crucial issues in the family are resolved and the most important advice given by a mother at this time. Jhumpi thought she could make some difference in her son's thinking. She needed him to know that she cares very much for him and that his sadness is tearing her heart apart.

"Son, you can't go on like this" – She said in a point blank voice.

Harish did not answer. He could not. But he realized that his mother was as sad as he was, maybe even more. She had seen more deaths in her life than he had. So she could understand it better and had developed an inborn mechanism to cope with it. For him, his mother was a perennial source of strength. Her strength came from her never ending love. Harish did not know how to respond or what to say. It appeared as if he was concentrating on eating without saying a word.

Jhumpi laid her right palm on her son's head. In a very heavy voice she told him" Son, Haru is not coming back. You need to get hold of yourself. You need to go on with life. The kids are upset. Your sadness kills them, kills everybody. Look, how thin you appear now. You can't go on like this."

"What do you want me to do?"

"You need to do all the usual things. You need to go back to Calcutta where you belong. For a man like you, this village does not have much to offer. You have friends there. Your clients look for you. They need you. You need them. After all the money you spent on Haru, you are broke now."

"In spite of being sad, mother has not forgotten all the practical things in life." he thought. By reminding him that he needed money she was pushing him in a very practical direction.

"Who is going to care for Sudha and Anand?"

"Look Sudha is a big girl now. While you are in Calcutta I will look for a good boy for her. The kind of beauty she is, she should have no problem in attracting a good match arranged by the family. I will look after them. When your father died I looked after you and your sister. Didn't I?"

"Yes, mother. You did a fantastic job" said Harish.

At the moment he was sad and weak. Haru's death, her permanent absence in his life, had created a deep void that was making him increasingly weak and sad. His mother's suggestion gave him strength. It always did. By mentioning his childhood his mother brought back some soothing memories for him. Her caring, loving words seemed to penetrate Harish's exhausted mind. He agreed with her. She was right. She always was. He decided that he had to return to Calcutta.

The night before he left his home in the village he hugged his children. He told Sudha to look after her grandmother and advised her to act like a responsible girl. He admonished Anand not to be naughty and always obey his grandmother. The children did not want him to leave. But they knew that it was necessary for daddy to go to Calcutta. He always did. "Calcutta" and "daddy" were synonymous in their thinking.

This time, Harish was not very enthusiastic about leaving his village. His heart was heavy and his mind exhausted. He wished he did not have to leave the village and his mother and his children. In a very mechanical way, he bade good bye to all of them and very early in the morning backtracked on the same road to the train station. On his way he stopped at the same shop to drink water and to have a snack. He crossed the same river and streams. He saw the same trees and crossed the same familiar fields where cows grazed and crops grew. At the end of his journey he reached the train station. By then the day was gone, and he was exhausted.

He rested on a vacant seat on a cement bench of the station and waited for the train that was due in three hours.

Finally the train arrived after dark. Its enormous sound and chugging and smoke seen from a long distance brought a sense of finality to his purpose. A ticket in hand, he boarded the train. Like him, there were many other anxious people who sat inside the train on wooden benches. Their sweaty bodies and bundles of luggage filled the compartment. With his own little bundle by his side, Harish became one of them. All the passengers were strangers to him and probably to each other. No one knew who was a thief or a pickpocket. So, each of them eyed the other with studied carefulness. Within an hour or so Harish bonded with some people in the compartment and struck up conversations. While the train moved, their conversation became friendly, sympathetic and full of opinions and suggestions. The passengers started talking about their children, their work, families, villages and life experiences. Harish joined them. He too opened up to the group of strangers around him. By telling his own story he felt relieved. He felt connected.

By the time the train arrived at Howrah station in Calcutta it was well into morning. The sky looked cloudy and dark. Occasional drizzle made everything miserably damp and muddy. Harish did not mind. Once again he was glad to be there. He did not mind the cloudy sky. His own mind and heart were extremely clouded and heavy.

11

While Harish was in the village attending to Haru's needs and then her funeral, Calcutta had gone through a sea change. There was tension in the air. People were afraid to go out in the dark. The fear was almost everywhere. Even the big, muscular men seemed to be afraid. There were rumors of killing in the neighborhoods, abduction of children on the streets and raping of women in their homes. Some of the stories were true. Some were not. Nevertheless, the stories were spinning uncontrollably. No one knew what to expect or how to overcome the situation. The cloud of fear was being spread out beyond the reach of common folks. What they were getting was bits and pieces of news tainted with the narrator's own slant on things.

For years, Calcutta's citizens had lived peacefully. Thanks to the British, it was the biggest city in the country. All kind of people --- people with money and education and land and positions lived there. Those who could write stories and poems made their home in Calcutta. So did the actors, singers, artists and teachers and publishers. All kinds of people from all over the country came to Calcutta to carve out a living. They came from all kind of religious backgrounds. Among those were Hindus who worshipped everything and whose religion made them identify with all kind of creatures. And they believed that God himself came down to Earth in different shapes and forms and did all kind of human things such as getting married, making babies and ruling a country. This sort of belief was strange to many of those who came to Calcutta for a visit or for business from the outside world. For example, right in the monsoon, the people of Calcutta would make statues of clay and worship them with all kind of fanfare. And in a couple of days the clay statues would be thrown into a body of water. A lot of people would join the procession to immerse a statue. The same would continue for a statue named Ganesh. It would have an elephant's head and a huge belly. Every school child would worship the statue only to throw it away in the water. Goddess Durga would be treated in the same way. Every nook and cranny of Calcutta worshipped the statue. It had ten hands, wore a crown and sat on the back of a lion. Thousands of people, rich and poor, educated and uneducated, would line up to worship an image that stayed only for three days. Then with a lot of pomp and ceremony the statue would be immersed in water. During the three days during "puja" a genuine festive atmosphere engulfed the city. People fasted and feasted; they exchanged gifts with friends and relatives. Every one tried to make the occasion pleasant and enjoyable. The mud on the ground, occasional drizzle, the chaos on the street – nothing bothered anyone. They loved the occasion.

Calcutta also had a few churches. Unlike the temples, the architecture of church buildings looked different. They had spires. Churches preached a very different religion that did not worship a god or a goddess. Hindus, the overwhelming majority of the people of Calcutta, did not understand the church or its business.

They studiously stayed away from it. The churches rang bells, ran schools and helped the poor and the sick. They also converted others. Those connected with the church ate beef like Muslims did.

For a Hindu, the Killing of a cow was unthinkable. It was supposed to be worshipped like a mother. The churchgoers were different. For them, a cow was an animal meant for food. So the ordinary folks thought that the beef-eaters were heathens who would never go to heaven.

The group that enjoyed a very different life style and was most familiar with the local custom was the Muslim community. Like any other corner of the country Calcutta had its Muslim pockets. In that respect Calcutta was not unique. There were many towns and villages where for generations Hindus and Muslims had been living together. They celebrated each other's festivities and holidays. They lived next door to each other. Yet, in certain cases they stayed like oil and water and never mixed.

Then there were Sikhs. The menfolk in this community kept a beard, did not cut their hair on their head; always covered it by a turban. They also wore an iron bangle around their right wrist. In most ways they acted like Hindus because Sikhism was a sect of Hinduism until recently, when some of the Sikhs started saying that theirs was a separate religion. They called their temple "Gurudwara". No form of meat was allowed to enter its premises. Their lifestyle was very much like that of the Hindus but in some ways they took radical stands in day- to- day living. They had no caste system and worshipped no statues. They seemed to be more hard working.

The Zoroastrians called "Parsis," were a very visible lot in Calcutta. All the big businesses seemed to belong to them. They worshipped the Sun. The women folk in the Parsi community were more outgoing, more educated and like their Christian counterparts did not mind walking alone on the street. Instead of burying or cremating their dead, the Parsis placed their dead in a tower in a walled-in field where vultures feasted on the body. For the dead, they believed, it was the final act of sacrifice.

Most of the people who lived in Calcutta belonged to these religions. Then there were many others who acted differently or were different. They were too few and their presence did not make much impact on anyone.

People from all over India came to Calcutta to make a living. For them the city was a garden of labor. They worked and got paid for their work and sent the money home where their wives, parents and children lived. Many of those working people felt uprooted. Because of their isolation from home and family they occasionally became a prey to the manipulation of others. That is exactly what happened in recent months in a very grand way.

While Harish was away in the village something had changed in Calcutta. Behind the calmness of day- to-day living, anger was brewing under the surface. A struggle for freedom was going on. He knew that the Sadhu from his village was one of the many who had gone to jail for his involvement in such a struggle. But the struggle for freedom was not very visible. Within the country and among the people there was fear everywhere now. Many with vested interests were encouraging hate. Hate was in the air. It also generated fear. As a result, both hate and fear became deeply rooted in people's psyche. A time came when neighbors in Calcutta started fearing neighbors. Not that there was any reason to do so. But those who wanted to make a profit from the situation started stoking the fire of fear and hatred in the hearts and minds of ordinary people who were mostly gullible and easier to be manipulated. This took the turn toward communal conflict. Slowly the situation became explosive. Communal violence was spreading. Neighbors representing Hindu and Muslim communities seemed to be suspicious of each other in most places. Within a few days Calcutta transformed into a burning inferno of communal hatred. Its atmosphere became poisonous. Things seemed to be happening beyond the grasp of ordinary people. As an insignificant nut in a big whirring machine each of its citizens seemed to be a helpless part in a process that was unfolding somewhere else. Yet, all of them were unmistakably feeling the pain from an ongoing tragedy.

Calcutta, at the time, was burning. Its streets had become a dangerous place. Groups of thugs had taken over. Vandals were roaming and shouting obscene epithets against certain individuals and communities. They carried a grudge. Women and children were the most vulnerable in a time like this. So, able-bodied family members in each family gathered every one into a safe corner in their respective houses and apartments. To save themselves from roaming thugs, many were hiding in the safest place of their dwellings. In some areas, men were clustering together to create a safe habitat for their wives, mothers, daughters and other female members of their families. The children looked scared. They could not understand yet saw vividly what was happening around them. It was difficult for them to know that an entire city had gone mad.

The tension had been building up for days and weeks. Shopkeepers on the street had already sensed that something was wrong and they had either left the area in fear or had closed and padlocked their shops. Because of their exodus from the city, foodstuffs like everything else, were in short supply. There was a war going on in Europe and the Far East and the government was taking everything away from its civilians to support its soldiers who desperately wanted to win the war encompassing the whole world.

There were looters in the streets. They broke into boarded up, padlocked stores and were supported and encouraged by knife wielding thugs. Who those thugs were or how they got there did not matter. Their presence in the city was a reality. The entire city seemed to be in flames. Life was miserable. Living in Calcutta was dangerous and unbearable at this time. Harish had no idea about all of these things. Because of Haru's death he was pretty emotionally beaten down. Now that he was in Calcutta he wanted to tend to his personal situation. He needed to get back to a daily routine that was familiar to him. But given the atmosphere in Calcutta such a routine became just a dream. As soon as he arrived in the city, life seemed to be going from bad to worse by the hour. Everybody was anxious and nobody knew when all this would end. There was a sense of desperation in the air.

What was happening on the streets was bad enough. But the stories flying in from all directions were even worse. He heard from a neighbor that a few blocks away two burly and bearded men chopped off the head of a bricklayer. The hapless guy's dead body reportedly lay on the street. There was a pool of blood on the concrete. The hoodlums took the man's tools and ran away. The man was a Hindu and his killers were not, he was told.

The person who told this story to Harish heard the story from someone who heard the story from someone else. What actually happened may or may not have been accurate, yet because of fear no one dared to check the incident. Harish was one of those who heard the story and was terribly afraid. His fear was mostly the reflection of the feelings of his neighbors. A few of them had young children and worried for their safety. They feared for their lives. In any conflict, especially in a communal conflict, the rape and molestation of women become common. The body of a woman from the opposite side represents all the powerlessness and vulnerability in the world and the miscreants exploit that weakness.

The beastly characters attack the women and let loose their own repressed desires. Everyone knew that it could happen now. Such a possibility was heart breaking. Grown men began to cry because they realized that in the face of an angry mob they were helpless to protect their women. Nothing was more shameful and unendurable than seeing one's daughter, sister or wife being violated. The men were determined to put up a fight to protect the honor of their women. They also knew that they could lose. But they collectively vowed to fight to the death. They theorized that dying would be better than living to remember such a horrible incident. Their determination gave them strength.

Very few of them had any weapons. Other than kitchen knives and a few bamboo sticks the residents of Harish's neighborhood had no tools to protect themselves physically. As the shouting became louder and louder outside, the people inside the neighborhood began to panic. At the same time none of them was willing to leave the area. The street had become dangerous. The surrounding area was unsafe now. At a time like this the number was important. Therefore, each of them wanted to become a part of a larger group. Staying alone was not going to help. So, no matter what, they wanted to stick together. Their combined numbers gave them strength. Because so many people were still around, the families with children felt a bit reassured.

Mothers and grandmothers hid themselves with their young daughters and granddaughters. In small apartments where clusters of them huddled together very few places were left unoccupied where they could go to hide. They had fear in their hearts and their eyes said it all. They did not know what was going to happen to them individually or collectively. The women in the neighborhood were worried. All their lives they had learned to be protected by their menfolk. But this was a different time. The men were unsure of their strength both individually and collectively in the face of an unknown danger. But they had faith in God. They prayed. In a very perverse way, they believed that one way or another, all the Gods in heaven were going to protect them. They had no idea as to how that was going to happen but they had faith in their belief.

Without knowing for sure exactly what was happening outside his immediate neighborhood Harish and his roommates began to worry. Harish thought of his mother and children. At this point he seemed to be more concerned about his children than himself. The children just lost their mother. "What would happen to them if I die?" He repeated this question millions of times in his mind. The more he thought about it the more he became worried and scared. He did not want to leave his children unprotected. He did not want his old mother to be responsible for taking care of them. "What would happen to her?" He kept asking. There seemed to be no answer. He prayed for his own safety. He prayed for the protection of his children. Praying came to him naturally. In times of trial he always prayed.

Momentarily, his happy years in Calcutta stood before him like a dream. Now he was faced with a stark reality whose meaning he could not understand. All he could decipher was that a group of murderous men were prowling the streets with total impunity. They wanted to kill and rob others. He could not understand why they were behaving in such a way. The Calcutta he knew did not harbor such people. Yet, they were there and now they were roaming everywhere, terrorizing everybody. And he could not fathom as to how he would survive the present situation. He felt helpless and he worried and prayed again and again.

Among the people who lived in the neighborhood of low rising houses where Harish lived, Sardar Singh always stood out. He had a thick mustache. His head was almost bald. He was fat and bulky. Sardar Singh's big stomach was the first thing people noticed about him. For whatever reason, he took it upon himself to help save everybody. He was a "bastiwalla" meaning he grew up in the rough and tumble of the neighborhood and he did not want to be intimidated by any one from outside. Sardar Singh wanted to act.

First of all, he took some friends with him and went house to house in his neighborhood to see that everyone was safe. Then he collected a group of men from the neighborhood. He did not have to ask them to come. As soon as they saw him the men came, one by one, automatically. Everyone called him "Sardar" meaning leader. He had no wife, no children. No one knew where he worked. But he was a longtime fixture in the neighborhood. Whenever there was a crisis or a conflict he intervened as if he felt obligated to do so. If the fighting erupted between two groups of rowdy boys then his was the final arbitration. If there was a dispute between a shopkeeper and a customer the aggrieved usually sought his intervention. Over a period of time – no one could correctly remember since when – he seemed to have ingratiated the entire neighborhood. So in a time like this his presence was reassuring. This was also a time when each head of the family was searching for a way out of this dangerous situation. People kept asking him   "What can we do? Something must be done." Other than his own presence among them Sardar Singh did not have anything solid to offer. For whatever reason they kept addressing the question to him. He had to give an answer to them and he did.

"Look brothers" Sardar Singh replied "We have to keep all of our front doors open. All the women and children have to be inside while all of the men must stay together in the yard. Any bastard who comes from outside gets a whack from all of us at the same time. That is how the buffaloes sleep in the open; each facing outward together."

It was a creative idea that gave the men a sense of security and everybody needed security at a time like this. Other than his own presence, Sardar Singh did not have anything else to offer. Yet, his presence among the scared people was a source of strength. For whatever reason, the people of the neighborhood trusted his strength and his judgment. As per his suggestion all of the men came out and gathered in the yard. Each of them held a weapon whatever came handy. Fighting with a weapon for any reason was not their practice. They were working men who tried to make a living. However, the circumstances now were different. They were about to be attacked and they had to defend themselves. When all of the men gathered together, Sardar Singh asked someone "How many men are here who live by themselves?" Someone gave him a few names including Harish's.

"Look guys, the situation is dangerous. I saw this morning what happened in Belgacchia. The bastards killed that poor bricklayer for no apparent reason. Hoodlums are prowling the streets. They are organized and they may come to attack us. If they do, then we have to fight back."

"Is there a safe place where we can hide?" asked someone.

"There is one place I know. But that place would hold only two people at the best. Besides where would the children and women go? They need our protection and all of us have to stay here. If we have to die then we will die together in the name of Bajrangwali." Every one spontaneously sang "Bajrangbali ki Jai. Glory to the Lord Hanuman. Sardar Singh cleared his throat and continued "I think two of the men should go to safety if they want to." At this point every one's eyes were fixed on Harish. He was a Brahmin and a priest. Therefore, everyone felt that it was his duty to keep him safe. The safe place turned out to be a manhole above a sewer line. In order to reach there which was a block away, Harish had to walk discreetly. The manhole had a cover which could be locked from inside. Harish felt uneasy leaving the group. Yet he did. With him came a man named Govind. When they came out together Harish did not know which place was safer, the place he left or the hole which he was going into.

It was dark. With Govind in front, Harish was glancing carefully in all directions. He knew about the manhole. It was not too difficult to find.

As an occasional pickpocket, Govinda possessed a special skill to locate things. With his brilliance, they did not have much difficulty raising the lid of the manhole in the dark. In fear for their lives they stepped into the dark hole gingerly. Govinda helped Harish to get into the hole. They could not see anything in the dark. So Govinda lit a matchstick. He always carried a matchbox with him for lighting his bidi.

Under the hole there were three steps about two feet wide and two feet deep. The steps led to a sewer line. The stench was horrible. But both men felt reasonably safe and gingerly put the lid back on.

There was hardly any room to lie down. In a sitting position they stayed up all night. From inside the hole they could hear noises in the street. They could hear voices of threats and counter threats and the wailing of women and children. Sounds of exploding firecrackers and burning houses kept coming. It was scary. But there was nothing the two men could do now. To avoid the chances of the wrong people picking up their conversation and discovering them hiding they could only whisper to each other to communicate. They stayed there to save their lives. Given the condition, the smell, the dinginess and darkness of the hole, they were not quite sure that they could survive there very long. Outside, the situation above ground was becoming ever increasingly dangerous. Given the ebb and flow of the noise both men were sure something very bad was happening.

Govinda had a few bundles of bidi, tiny cigarettes rolled in a leaf and filled with tobacco. He could forego food for days. But without a bidi he was totally helpless. Nervously, he tried to light one of his bidis. Harish did not smoke. He became concerned that the smoke of the bidi might pass through the lid and might cause them to be discovered. Govinda saw the logic. And very sadly he gave up his smoking. Harish had a few betel leaves filled with betel nut and spices. It was a stimulant but one had to develop a taste for it because it is actually awful in taste. Govinda never liked to chew this substance called paan. But he took one from Harish and chewed nervously. Both Harish and Govinda were scared. The very thought of incidents taking place above ground made them nervous.

In the darkness of the hole, Govinda whispered to his companion" Do you think, we can survive?"

"It is all in God's hands" replied Harish. He did not want to sound fatalistic. But he had no answer. Putting everything in God's hands was easy and it took him off the hook. Govinda halfheartedly accepted the answer and showed no emotion about it. "I am the only son of my mother. She is getting old. If I die, I don't know who is going to care for her." Govinda broke down and sobbed. At that very moment, Harish thought of his mother and children. He just wished that he would be able to go back to them. Harish knew Govinda was not married. But this was not the time to ask personal questions. Their survival was at stake. They were hiding to save their lives. He just told Govinda in a very calm and hushed voice "You have to get hold of yourself. We are hiding. No one knows what is waiting for us. In a situation like this we have to keep our minds sharp and clear." Govinda understood. On the back of his hand he wiped water from his eyes.

Evening became night and the night gave way to a bright day. But Govinda and Harish remained holed up above the sewer line. They had very little food and water with them and shared whatever they had. Neither of them was really hungry. Both the men just lay down on the dirty concrete steps with no desire to sleep or get up.

Sporadic noise from outside continued for quite some time. It was hard to tell how many hours or how many days passed. In that dark dingy tunnel Harish and Govinda lost count. All they could hear was the wailing of women and children, the shouting of the angry mobs, the crackling of burning houses and the firing of guns and bursting of firecrackers. And they had no idea as to who was doing what to whom.

Slowly the noise outside died down. And it followed by an utter calm. "Maybe everything is alright outside" – commented Govinda.

"Maybe we should wait a bit longer to be sure everything is okay" replied Harish. And they did.

All of a sudden they heard the sound of heavy police boots. At a regular interval this sound of boots continued at the same spot. Metal soles made a heavy and reassuring sound. "Maybe it is quiet now because of the police." Harish said.

In the speculation that they could come out, Harish and Govinda talked in a voice that was slightly louder than before. Two policemen were walking above ground and they heard the voice. While the two men were holed up underground the situation in Calcutta was causing havoc all over India. On the one hand people were trying to be free. On the other hand they could not get along. Those who were in charge of managing the country could not figure out what to do. Finally, the military came to town and tried to keep order. "Keep calm or we will shoot you" was their message and people were forced to listen to them. After a fully blown riot in the city, somehow peace prevailed. There was plenty of anger and distrust among its inhabitants. But the goons and thugs could not get a free hand anymore because of the military. There was a curfew and they could not roam the streets. Two of the military policemen overhearing the conversation belonged to that group. "I think some one is hiding somewhere" One of them told the other. Then they saw the big metal cover on the side of the road and pulled it up. Two heads showed up. Harish and Govinda looked up. They saw two men dressed in military uniforms looking at them. The uniformed men had guns. "Please don't shoot us. We are innocent," Govimda and Harish shouted from their hole. They feared for their lives. For the first time, they were face to face with a gun.

"Get off your ass and come here," ordered one of the military men. Harish and Govinda could hardly get up. After so many hours of sitting without food or water and being bitten by millions of mosquitoes day and night they hardly had any strength. Yet, slowly they left their hiding place and came above ground.

After a few minutes of questioning the military men realized that the two men were genuinely hiding for their lives and were innocent. When they learned about the men's neighborhood they became visibly upset. "That was the worst hit neighborhood. Every one is dead there. All the houses went up in flames." There was a moment of deafening silence between them. No one spoke. All four of them were standing. All of a sudden Harish's head started reeling. He sat down.

12

Like a wounded bird looking for its nest, Harish had no choice but to return to his village. He had no money or luggage to take home. The train station and the train compartments were full of people who were returning home with only the clothes on their backs. All of them suffered the impact of the communal riot. Each of them had a story to tell. And one common thread that linked all of them together was their skill to survive. They had saved themselves from a very harrowing situation. Having lost everything, none of them knew now what lay ahead. At this point, being broke did not matter. They were thankful to be alive.

While traveling with others in a packed compartment, Harish was forced to hear quite a few horror stories. One of the passengers named Madhu survived by pretending to be dead. He was traveling in a rickshaw. A bunch of goons came upon him from nowhere. They attacked the rickshaw puller by hitting him on the head with bamboo sticks. The man fell on the street and let out a deafening scream. It was probably his scream of an instant death. The rickshaw, without its driver, veered into a ditch. Madhu, the passenger, fell in the ditch and the rickshaw lay on top of him. He had seen what happened to the rickshaw driver. He too expected a similar fate. So he pretended as if he was dead. After giving a big scream he lay very still. It was too much work for the goons to lift the rickshaw and beat a dead man underneath. So they left. After lying there in the ditch for hours until dark, Madhu finally got up and scanned the street carefully and was convinced that there was no one around. So he walked up to a temple, some distance away. A group of men had gathered there and for the time being this temple became everyone's safe haven.

Then there was Khatua, a very thin man with a long nose. All other days for work. A group of men came upon him, snatched his bag, kicked him and hit him. They left him unconscious on the road. He had no idea about how he survived or who took care of him when he was unconscious. The only thing he knew was that he was surrounded by a group of policemen when he woke up. They helped him to the train.

A handful of passengers had made deliberate attempts to be safe and took precautions. Some of them had planned for their safety and were successful in avoiding communal danger. Yet many were not so lucky. Danger just fell upon them. They became victims of a situation that they did not create and did not know how to end. They perished at the hands of goons and miscreants.

Some of the passengers survived owing to sheer luck. In the face of a violent mob that was out to kill and maim at will, each of those men sitting in the train compartment now was powerless at that time. The men had nothing to fight with. They were not even prepared to fight. They applied their brains to survive. They were thankful that they did not die.

"Someone must be watching over me," each of them thought. For the time being their shared experiences made each of them a believer.

In Harish's way of thinking they did not die because their time was not up yet.

"In the nature of things, everything has a predetermined place for itself. Death, birth, good, bad, all of the earthly things are predisposed to a decision made in heaven long before they actually take place. This is called God's will, so they survived." He expressed himself in a thankful and fatalistic way. He remembered several stanzas from scriptures written thousands of years ago in Sanskrit. They all said the same thing about God and His will.

The train was packed like a can of sardines. There were too many people in the compartment. It was hot outside and hotter inside the car known as a buggy. The doors and windows were open and the air from outside made sitting relatively comfortable. The travelers were sweating. Their sweaty bodies discharged a pungent odor. Yet, the body odor did not matter. They were all in the same boat. Their shared experience of almost certain death tied them together and they chatted away with each other as if they had been friends for ages.

Through the windows of the train, Harish could see the endless expanse of the dark and cloudy sky. Occasionally, puffs of air filled with coal dust and sand smeared his body. In exhaustion he dozed off. In the train, travelers usually stay awake to keep their belongings safe from pickpockets and thieves. However, in this train no one seemed to have any material thing that a thief would want. There were no thieves. They were all survivors.

Hours passed. Between the conversation with his fellow travelers and his dozing off the journey finally ended around daybreak. He got off the train and began walking home. He remembered his journey to the village the last time; he was anxious for Haru's health. This time there would be no Haru waiting for him. He wished she was alive today but she was not. And he wanted to be with her.

"No. It is not possible. Besides, I have things to do for Sudha and Anand. I can't follow Haru. Not now." Harish listened to his thoughts. They seemed to be sad and overwhelming.

The distance from the railroad station to his home in the village was quite long and it required hours of walking. During that lengthy walk he had a lot to think about. Things that he did or conversations he had with people in the past rose and fell in his mind. His childhood, his youth and his life in Calcutta, all of them, came alive in his memory. He shuddered at the thought of the inferno he had just left behind.

While thinking about the past, Harish could not see a bright future for him. It looked dark and unsettling. In Calcutta he performed Puja and people gave him money. With cash in his hands he could buy things and send money home. Now the city was ruined. Tens of thousands of people fled the city. He lost his friends and clients. The possibility of his going back to Calcutta again was remote. He knew he could not live in the village to do farming or business. Farming was too hard and unreliable. It needed hard work of the physical kind. Then there was the risk of a flood and drought. Harish knew that he could not handle that kind of work. Neither could he run a business. First of all, going into business required a mindset, a way of thinking that he did not have. He could not say 'no' to people who would buy things on credit with no intention to pay back, ever. He had never run a business of any kind. And he did not feel confident that he could start now. In order to make a living, he wanted to go away to some place other than Calcutta.

That exploration would come later. But for Harish the problem at hand right now was getting home. Through the narrow streams, sandy river beds, barren fields and village-roads he had to walk and keep walking. When he became tired he rested under a tree. If walking in the hot sun made him thirsty, he stopped near a well and drew some water and drank. On his way home, he stopped by a roadside shop where he ate some puffed rice and curd.

By the time Harish reached home he was tired and exhausted. His feet were smeared with dust. He was happy to see his children and his mother.

The news of riots in Calcutta somehow had reached the village and Jhumpi had been praying for her son's safety. Now that he was actually home safely her joy and happiness was boundless. From the bottom of her heart, she thanked all the Gods and Goddesses she could remember. She bowed to them over and over for keeping him safe. Sudha and Anand were elated to see their father. The house momentarily filled with joy. Harish hugged his son and daughter and bowed to his mother. Now, being in his village and with his family, Harish momentarily forgot all that walking and exhaustion. He was happy.

Since Haru's death, a veil of sadness hung over the family. Often, Anand would cry in his sleep for his mother. When awakened by a dream he would ask for her. Very carefully hiding from her grandmother, Sudha at times would weep for her mother. Yet, she would pay attention to her brother's needs. The little boy at times threw terrible tantrums. His grandmother was too old to run after him. He was too precocious and the old lady was frail and weak. But he listened to his older sister.

Anand needed his father. Now that he was home Sudha felt assured. Jhumpi on her part was concerned for her son. She knew how much her son loved Haru. Her death was a big blow to him. No one could ever replace Haru. She was so lovable. Jhumpi herself missed Haru day and night. In her own heart' Jhumpi did not want Haru to be replaced by any one if she could help it.

The harrowing experience in Calcutta during the riot had taken an emotional toll on Harish. Now, without Haru, the home felt empty. He could not sleep at night. For hours, night after night, he stayed awake in bed while years of memories passed through his head. In the darkness and in his mind Haru's beautiful face came alive. He felt the soft touch of her body. He could even smell the jasmine oil from her hair. Haru always used jasmine oil in her hair when she came to bed, he remembered. A few drop of tears would roll from the corners of his eyes. He would realize that Haru was gone forever. A sense of despair would come upon him. After tossing and turning in bed for hours he would fall asleep.

The next morning, he would wake up into a bigger vacuum in his existence.

Every morning he would wake up to a sunny day and do his errands. In the river he would dip in its cold and clear water. He would walk in the fields of rice and legume. The lush green leaves of the farmed crops would give him joy. The yellow mustard flowers and the white coriander flowers stretched for miles before him. Millions of bees would be buzzing around and collecting honey. Harish enjoyed their buzzing. Often, he visited with some of his old pals in the village. At times, they came to see him. He could sense that everyone felt sorry for him because of his wife's death. After a while visiting friends became a drag. How long can he take the same sorrow in their voices? Instead of visiting friends he developed a habit of taking long walks, alone. Sometimes if Anand was home after school he took the boy with him.

It was fun for Anand. The flowers, the bees, the birds, and the vegetables were all new to him. Each of them had a different smell and size and color. "What is that?" "Why is this" were his set of questions. The inquiring mind of a child wanted answers to everything. He asked those questions to his father continuously.

His young son's inquiring mind gave Harish a new energy to think. While walking with him and answering his questions he himself could look back at his own childhood. Harish could not remember his days with his own father who died when Harish was very young. Now that he was able to spend time with his own son it made him very happy. "One day, hopefully, the boy would remember his days with his father," thought Harish.

The time in the village seemed to pass slowly and painfully. He felt he was a misfit. Yet, he had nowhere else to go. It was his village. So he tried to make the best of his being there. In the village the days were long and work was hard. Whatever work one did to survive was done manually with or without a tool. He knew how to chant a sloka and perform a puja. He was content to read and meditate for hours. Those were wrong kind of skills to survive in his village now.

One day, while sitting on his porch on a palm-leaf-mat and looking at the sunset Harish was in his usual mood of melancholy. His mother approached him from inside the house. She had been separating stones from the lentils. "Son, Are you thinking about your daughter or not?" Jhumpi asked him without any preamble. Harish gave her a blank look. She repeated again "Look, the girl is 16. She should be ready to have her own world now. You have to look for a suitable boy for her. You need to think of her wedding"

Harish had not given much thought about Sudha's wedding. To him she was still   "daddy's little girl". Right after Haru's death he was emotionally numb and could not address any serious matters. A daughter's wedding required not only finding a suitable groom but dowries for his family and feasts for the relatives. All this required money. He was not a rich man. But he was rich enough to find the necessary means to marry his daughter off into a good family. He lacked the required strength to put things together. The authority in his mother's voice now put some urgency to the matter. "God willing, it will happen very soon" replied Harish. The way he said it, Jhumpi got a very clear indication that her words had their necessary effect on him. Then she went inside to separate stones from the lentils..

A few days later Harish found a prospective son in law. The young man Dinesh, a.k.a Dinu, was a school- teacher. His father owned a few acres of land that provided his family its annual needs of rice and lentils. The family lived in a flood affected area. Therefore, the annual harvest was never a sure thing. But Chandra Acharya, the patriarch of the family, managed his land well. If the crop of rice was lost due to floods in the monsoon season then to compensate the loss he grew legumes after the monsoon. Anyway, Chandra too was looking for a bride for his son. And he knew about Harish. Chandra was very happy to make Harish his son's father in law.

When a wedding takes place, it solemnizes the relationship between a man and a woman by making them husband and wife. Within the tradition of the village life, it permanently cements a relationship between two families and they become each other's relatives. Therefore, compatibility between the families becomes important.   "The wedding" becomes a business of common worship, giving gifts and taking presents. At every step of the way, shrewd negotiation takes place. To an outsider the sequence of worship, the exact time for the ceremony and the color of the Sari for the bride may seem meaningless. But in rural areas where tradition and custom rule every aspect of life, each of this issue becomes extremely important. During a wedding, every family, rich or poor, more or less goes through this process. Harish was ready in his mind. Yet, at the same time he toyed with the idea that Sudha should choose her own husband. He theorized in his mind that every young man and woman should choose his or her own partner. Boys and girls should meet and talk and if they clicked with each other then they should marry. This had happened in ancient times. "Why not now?" he would ask himself. There would be no answer. And he would change his thinking.

The Acharyas and the Mishras finally agreed on an auspicious day for the wedding of Sudha and Dinu. Negotiations for a dowry, the number of people coming in the groom's party and other issues took place in the courtyard of the village temple. The Gods of the temple became witnesses to the agreement between them. And each party, based on its interpretation of the agreement, was bound to its words. It was an arranged marriage in a village. And all the arrangements and negotiations took place between and among the relatives and family members. Two fathers and assorted uncles, cousins and relatives were involved. Neither the bride nor the groom had much to say in the matter. Everyone was looking after the welfare of both of them. As a result they had little to say on their own. It was neither polite nor necessary to have independent thinking in such an important thing like getting married. "The elders know the best" was the thinking and it was true. Such an arrangement had been continuing for as long as one could remember. So the system of "arranged marriage" was strong and effective.

Jhumpi was thrilled about the forthcoming wedding. She was happy for her granddaughter and the man she was about to marry. The young man came from a good family and had gone to school and was polite. All of this impressed Jhumpi. She thought Dinu was a perfect match for Sudha. She praised Harish for finding such a handsome young man for his daughter.

Sudha, on her part, did not seem to know what to expect. She had seen girls in her village get married. When the groom came with his party, havoc spread everywhere. A long ceremony and a lot of feasts took place. The girl after the ceremony said good bye to all her relatives and friends. She cried and wept. Everyone cried with her. Then she left for her in-laws' house. The girl became a woman by getting a husband.

As soon as Sudha thought of the word "husband", she felt a sensation within her. She instantly thought of Dinesh whom she had not yet met. A lot of thoughts about him came into her mind at once. Unconsciously she imagined him in many different ways, long nose, long arms, long hair and a round face. She imagined her head resting on his hairy chest. She imagined herself massaging his feet in the darkness of the night. Awkwardly, she thought of making love to him. She did not know what Dinesh looked like. Yet, in her mad imagination she imagined herself lying next to him blissfully naked. With all kinds of anxieties and thoughts in her mind, she nervously waited for the wedding to happen.

Harish, on his part, was both happy and sad. For him it was a happy moment because the little girl who used to sit on his knee was to get married now. She was going to radiate another family, another household with her presence. She would participate in the continuing saga of a family tree. One day, because of Sudha, he would have grandchildren and great grand children. He imagined in his mind how happy Haru would have been to see their daughter getting married. He missed her presence. As a father, he was trying to do all the right things for the occasion. Yet, inside him he was hurting badly because his wife was not there to share with him such a joy.

Finally, the day of the wedding arrived. The groom came to his in-laws' house. The grand ceremony took place under a make shift canopy of banana leaves. There was a display of firecrackers by the groom's party. And there was a grand feast. Every one seemed to be happy and it was a genuine occasion of happiness. When the wedding ceremony was over and the bride was declared to be the daughter in law of her new family, Sudha and Dinu from that moment on became a "couple". Harish was overwhelmed with feelings and broke down.

In the scheme of things, Sudha had to enter into a new life. She had to make her own nest. As a father, Harish had to help her fly to that new territory. He understood the reality.

Sudha bade good bye to her family and friends. In a cart drawn by a pair of bullocks she was driven to her new home where her in-laws waited to welcome her. Jhumpi and Harish gave their blessings and wept at her departure. And they were happy.

13

His daughter's wedding was over. The guests left and the house felt empty. At home and in the village, time for Harish passed in its usual way. He seemed to have reached a dead end. He did his errands and morning walks and visited the homes of friends. He had no agenda. He had no schedule. He felt restless and antsy. As days went by in this manner, he slowly began to realize that he had to find another pasture. He told this to his mother. She did not protest. She knew that life in the village was harsh and her son could not manage there for long.

Sudha used to do all the chores inside the house - small but important things like sweeping the porch and lighting the oil lamp for the evening. After the wedding, she left for the home of her in-laws. This work fell on Jhumpi and she resented it. She had not cooked a meal or used a broom in the house for many years. Haru used to do all the work inside the home. When she died,

Sudha kind of took over her mother's role. She was old enough and smart.

Harish did not mind doing chores in the house to help his mother. But he was a man. Working outside the home and bringing food for the family was his job. Jhumpi did not want him to be tied down to the cooking and cleaning. She tried to do those jobs as best as she could. Harish felt sorry for his mother but he could not change things as they were. He was reconciled to the fact that this was his fate. According to his horoscope, it was the unfavorable alignment of stars that caused him all the misfortune.

After a lot of thinking, Harish decided to go to Varanasi, known earlier as Benaras. Situated on the bank of the Ganges it was an ancient city full of temples and Sadhus. For every Hindu, Varanasi was a holy place. Years ago, Harish had visited there. From his village, it seemed to be much farther than Calcutta but Calcutta was ruined. After the traumatic experience of near death, he could not go back there. Varanasi offered him an alternative. He did not know anyone there but he strongly believed in his ability to make friends. Harish did not anticipate any problem in carving out a living in Varanasi. After consulting astrological charts, on the early morning of an auspicious day, Harish left his village for Varanasi. He went to the same train station that he knew for all of these years. From there he took a train and at a certain point he had to switch to another one.

Unlike other passengers, Harish was in no hurry to disembark at his destination. In the train he had plenty of time to think about how he was going to start his life in Varanasi. He knew that thinking about something was quite different from making it actually happen. So he was apprehensive but determined to make it work in his favor.

After arriving in the holy city he stayed for a few days in the waiting area of the train station. He had no apartment and no address. Other than a desire to make a living, he had no idea. Harish was a skilled palmist and a knowledgeable astrologer. He was sure that he would not have a shortage of patrons or clients.

Since he did not know the city, he needed time to scout a proper place to hang his hat. All he wanted to do was sit on a mat on a sidewalk with his hand written, cardboard sign: PALMIST. He was sure that once the word got around – about which he had no doubt- all kinds of people would come rushing toward him. Every one believed in fate. And each of them wanted to know what lay ahead and how the alignment of stars affected him or her. They also sought ways to overcome the wrath of the stars and the divine powers. Harish could help them in their search. At this point he himself was suffering from the wrath of stars. By reciting mantras and by chanting bhajans, he was trying to pacify them every day. As a blessing from the gods, he was able to carve out a corner of the waiting area of the train station as his living space. There were others.

The waiting area was officially built for transit passengers. It was the property of the railways. But Varanasi was a holy city. And all kinds of Holy men, the Sadhus of all shapes and sizes came and went through the station. No one ever questioned them. For them buying a ticket to travel was optional. Some of the men were elderly and others were not so old. Some had shaved their heads. Some holy men had long beard. A number of them were awfully heavy and some were extremely thin. Some of the holy men, with only loin clothes, looked almost naked. With beads around their necks some of them wore sandal paste on their foreheads. They worshipped different deities and all of them seemed to have disciples in the area. At times, some of them made the train station their temporary residence. The Sadhus, as the holy men were called, did not have a home in the usual sense of the term. Each of them had years ago left the security of a home or a home life. By renouncing such a comfort and worldly possessions they were living off the handouts. They were applying their thoughts for the betterment of mankind. In a way it was necessary and they thought it was.

Harish made friends with some of them. Some of the Sadhus had rich disciples settled in Varanasi who had built temples and rest houses for devotees and visitors. As businessmen, government contractors, landlords and professionals they had made enough money and now they could spend their spare change for charity. They looked after the holy men whom they considered their gurus. Harish became a friend with several Sadhus whose disciples made sure that he had enough to eat. His knowledge of palmistry also helped.

In addition to the Sadhus, the people who regularly came to know the details of their luck by letting him analyze the lines on their palms became acquaintances and some of them became his friends. In the meantime, Harish carved out a space on one side of a busy intersection. Day after day he became a fixture there. His familiar presence at his regular spot and the handwritten cardboard sign brought him customers and cash. He badly needed both.

Varanasi was not a big city like Calcutta. Calcutta had its Howrah Bridge. All kinds of people and carts ran over it. In Calcutta people swarmed like flies all the time. But the character of Varanasi was different. It had the famous temple for Lord Shiva. There were more Sadhus and Sanyasis per yard in Varanasi than any place anywhere. The air was filled with religion. He cherished the holiness of the Ganges and took a dip in the holy river every morning. Hundreds of others too came to take a dip in the Ganges. By doing so they thought they were washing off their sins. Yet, by congregating in large numbers and throwing objects into the river they were also helping to pollute the water.

Eventually, Harish rented a small room near a temple not very far from the holy river. After taking a dip in the river every morning he walked home while reciting stanzas from the Bhagabad-Gita. The utterance of different words in Sanskrit, sometimes clustered together, carried different meanings and the meanings stuck to his heart. Recitation made him happy. He felt peaceful within. This seemed to be the most enjoyable moment for Harish.

At the beginning, he was apprehensive about Varanasi but

after a month or two he began feeling confident that he could earn a living here. As proof of his ability he sent some money to his mother. Hindi was the prevailing language inVaranasi. He learned to speak like the locals very quickly. Learning a new language came to him naturally. He enjoyed languages. But English? That was another matter. For him English was the language of foreigners. He would have liked to learn it but he was not keen on it as he seemed to have an inner fear about this language whose construction and spelling did not follow the fixed design of any Indian language. He enjoyed Sanskrit. Its crisp pronunciation always inspired him.

Harish enjoyed reading Kalidas as well as Upanishads. He remembered that as a young man he used to enjoy Kalidas' poems very much. The great poet described his characters in the way only Kalidas could describe them. It was unique. Whenever he read them in later years he used to think of Haru. Since her death he stopped reading Kalidas because the great poet's epics made him sad. For inner cleansing and for inner strength he read the Upanishads and The Bhagabad-Gita instead. This ancient literature, considered holy by the Hindus, had a purifying effect on him. He was convinced that the reading of the Upanishads and the Bhagabad Gita offered him something that no other book could offer. It was inner peace he was looking for and he was convinced that the Gita and the Upanishads gave him the tools to get that.

As guardians of religious beliefs and practices the Sadhus, influenced the life and thinking in Varanasi. After being there for a while, Harish was inspired to observe his religion more aggressively. He lived on a vegetarian diet, spent several hours a day reciting scriptures and worshipped Gods and Goddesses regularly. In addition, he fasted on special occasions. At times he wished he were one of the Sadhus who seemed to have no fear and no worries. He was attracted to their ascetic life. Becoming a Sadhu also meant leaving family and home. The concept was alluring but he could not bring himself to doing it. He could not leave his family; not now anyway.

One morning, after taking his dip in the Ganges, Harish felt feverish. He thought it was something minor and would go away. He usually ate a bowl of cereal for breakfast. Because of the fever he did not feel like eating that day. Yet, he went to work. Like days before, he sat at his usual place to read palms on the sidewalk. The day was hot. But he felt a chill in his bones. He could not sit for long and felt like lying down. So he walked back to his little room and lay there, sick.

Medical treatment was an unfamiliar practice for ordinary people. They usually tried to ward off diseases with the help from medicine men selling traditional medicine of roots, barks, leaves, flowers and other things. They tried to help the sick. But their help could go only so far. The medicine men's knowledge of the mechanism of the body was limited. Based on personal experience and guess they treated their patients. Sometimes it worked and sometimes it did not.

Harish took some medicine but his fever did not diminish. He thought he would purify his body by fasting. After a day of fasting he felt very weak. Then he thought by drinking some milk he would gain back his strength but his stomach would not hold it. As soon as he drank a little bit of milk he was ready to throw up and he did. He became progressively weak and sick. When his misery did not end in a week, he became concerned for himself. Until now he was thinking that this sickness was a temporary setback and if he rested and ate properly he would be cured. He was wrong.

One of the Sadhus visited Harish and on seeing him sick offered him some powdered roots and barks of a medicine tree grown in the jungles of the Himalayas. Looking at his symptoms, the sadhu was convinced that the powder he was giving would cure Harish because it had cured others from more serious illnesses. For Harish, the Sadhu's prescription was a ray of hope. Both the visit and the medicine made him feel stronger. However, the relief was temporary and his illness did not really go away. Once again he continued to feel sick and lay on his bed shaking and shivering. The Sadhu's medicine had no effect on him and his fever continued making him weaker by the hour. Finally he decided to return home to his village which meant a long journey on a train and hours of walking from the train station to the village.It was a two full weeks of lying on his mat that finally convinced him to leave Varanasi and return home.

At this point Harish had a fear that he was going to die and he did not want to die in a strange place like Varanasi. If die he must, then he wanted to die among family members, friends and relatives. He needed to see his mother. So, worried about his impending death he wanted to go to his village.

Varanasi was the famous holy place. Many thought that by dying there one went to heaven directly. Bodies burnt in holy pyre were thrown into the holy river, the Ganges. Harish did not want his body to be thrown into a river even if the river was the Ganges. He wanted his body to be cremated in the graveyard of his tiny village where he grew up. For him, the shape of heaven was his village and after his death, from above the veil of clouds, he wanted to see the continuous change in its fields and trees that the seasons brought. The fear of dying made him very close to his village. It was a feeling of romance he had never felt before.

Harish finally boarded a train to go home. It was quite a journey. From the start he had a strange feeling that he would not be able to make it to the last station in the journey. But he did. All the while he was aching and shivering inside. He had wrapped a blanket around him. The passengers at various points would ask him "Brother, Are you okay? You look very sick". He would answer affirmatively. Since they were traveling from point A to point B and were busy with their own problems they could do very little. Besides, Harish did not expect any service from his fellow passengers. Their sympathy however, was reassuring for him.

After much pain and apprehension he finally reached the destination and from there he had to walk. This time he had no strength to walk. So he hired a bullock cart to carry him home. The driver of the cart was a nice man. By looking at Harish he realized that the man needed help. Without haggling for a fare, which was the usual practice, he agreed to drive him to his village.

Two strong bullocks were yoked to the cart. Each animal had bells around its neck. Together they made a jingling sound as they moved. The cart had a roof over it. The driver spread some straw on the floor of the cart. Harish lay on the straw. His body was aching and he was feeling really bad. At the same time he was trying to sleep. But the road had too many potholes and every time the cart hit one of them his bones rattled. It was impossible for him to sleep

At irregular intervals the driver would ask Harish about his condition and offer his services. At this point, all Harish wanted was to get home and rest.

Finally, it was evening and he was home in his village. Harish was relieved to see his son and his mother. But Jhumpi felt horror. She did not expect her son to come home so sick. She spread a clean sheet for him and he reclined on his usual mat. Then she prepared food that he always liked. But this evening Harish was exhausted and not hungry. He did not feel like eating. He let Anand sit near him and asked him some questions. Anand answered him as best as he could. Harish was the least interested in the correctness of his answers. He just wanted his son to talk to him. Anand's voice brought him happiness that he so desperately needed. But the happiness did not last too long. His head began to throb and he felt tired. Then, in the middle of Anand's explanation he brought his head down to the pillow and tried to sleep. He looked very tired. Anand could not figure out what was going on. In his child's mind he could sense that something was awfully wrong. But he did not know how serious the situation was. He could see the grimace on his father's face and the utter sadness in the face of his grandmother. He just wanted to be happy with his father and looked forward to going with him for a walk.

The next day the village medicine man, summoned by Jhumpi, came to the house.

He checked Harish's pulse, tongue and pupils. A sense of

worry permeated the medicine man's face. Before leaving the house he gave some powder from the barks and roots of a medicine plant. He told Jhumpi how long to boil them and how often to serve the medicine. "The patient is very sick" he said. There was concern in his voice and it made Jhumpi worried to death.

Over the years she had invested everything in her son. In a way, he was the reason for her existence in this world. She wanted good health and good fortune for him. But both fortune and health seemed to be slipping away from under his feet. First, he lost his wife. Then his career in Calcutta was ruined and he barely escaped there with his life. The illness hit while he was trying to establish himself in another place. "Why is the world so unkind to me?" she wondered aloud.

Jhumpi continued to give her son the boiled liquid as prescribed by the medicine man. In order to help him gain strength she continued to make some of his favorite dishes. She even modified her recipe so that he would find her dishes palatable. Days went by. Harish did not get better. Neither the medicine nor the care and prayer Jhumpi offered, brought Harish back to health. His condition became increasingly worse and increased her despair. She did not know what to do. Day and night, she cried a lot and prayed a lot but Harish's health did not change for the better. Her son's condition became so bad that he could not get up from bed any more. His eyes became sunken. His body became only skin and bones. He needed help to get up from his bed and Jhumpi was barely strong enough to help him. But she did. She resented the situation where she had to help her grown son out of bed. She would have been very happy if it would have happened the other way around. She considered this to be God's utter cruelty against her. She wanted to change things. But there was nothing she could do. Like a worm that finds shelter in its own shell, Jhumpi crawled into her own thoughts. They were painful. As her son's condition worsened, Jhumpi sent for Sudha.

As soon as she learned about her father's illness Sudha and her husband came to see him. Upon seeing them, Harish smiled at them and tried to get up to hug his daughter and son- in- law. He had not seen them since their wedding. Sudha looked so beautiful and so grown up. He tried to get up but could not. He was in pain. His smile gave way to a grimace and he fell onto his bed.

Sudha massaged her father's feet. They were swollen. She had never seen him so sick and so emaciated. Now she was not sure if he could pull through. She had lost her mother and she did not want to lose her father. The possibility of it made her very sad and scared. She was concerned for Anand also.

Sudha saw that her grandmother had given up eating and was weeping all the time. She could not bring herself to saying anything to her grandmother. Both of them shared the same grief but in different ways, one as a daughter and the other as mother.

Harish's illness brought grief to the entire village. The neighbors wanted to help. But there was nothing any of them could do other than visiting and consoling the family. For many, it was hard to believe that the medicine was not working.

Over the years, Harish and his mother had helped many of the neighbors and they all looked up to him in an adoring way. Now that he was ill they felt sorry for him. They were concerned about Jhumpi and Anand. The grandmother was too old to take care of herself and the boy was too young. Both the child and his grandmother needed protection for their survival. Harish was a good man and none of the neighbors wanted him to die.

"Why do bad things happen to good people?" they kept asking themselves. There was no answer. Yet, the bad thing did not stop.

Harish, on his part, seemed to be tired of fighting his illness. He did not want to die. But he did not want to keep on fighting endlessly, forever. In the condition he was in, the loss of will to fight against an ailment, turned out to be fatal for him.

One particular night when the darkness outside was quite deep and the village lay asleep in its collective grief, a heartbreaking wail pierced the silence. Sudha and Jhumpi and Anand were crying. The neighbors rushed in and the entire neighborhood woke up to see what happened. They gathered at the house. Harish's lifeless body lay on the bed. Failing to get better from whatever ailment he had, he finally succumbed to death. There was no hospital and no doctor. No one knew exactly what ailment took Harish's life. The neighbors gathered at the house. They mourned and wept. It was useless to console Jhumpi in a time like this and they let her cry as they knew, she the grieving mother, would continue to cry the rest of her life.

For the rest of the night the dead man's body lay on the bed surrounded by family and friends. After sunrise Harish was taken to the village cemetery like generations before him. There, with a ceremony his body was set on the pyre. From that moment on, melted into heaven, Harish became a memory for everyone and for ever.